WALLY MAMMOTH
Hide-and-Seek

BY **Corey R. Tabor**   PICTURES BY **Dalton Webb**

GREENWILLOW BOOKS
An Imprint of HarperCollins*Publishers*

For Will, who loves to be found
—C.R.T.

To Mom and Dad, who encouraged
me to seek my artistic path
—D.W.

HarperCollins Children's Books,
a division of HarperCollins Publishers
195 Broadway, New York, NY 10007

HarperCollins Publishers, Macken House,
39/40 Mayor Street Upper, Dublin 1, D01 C9W8, Ireland

Greenwillow Books is an imprint of HarperCollins Publishers.

Wally Mammoth: Hide-and-Seek
Text copyright © 2026 by Corey R. Tabor
Illustrations copyright © 2026 by Dalton Webb
All rights reserved. Manufactured in Capriate San Gervasio, Italy.
No part of this book may be used or reproduced in any manner whatsoever without written permission except in the case of brief quotations embodied in critical articles and reviews. Without limiting the exclusive rights of any author, contributor, or the publisher of this publication, any unauthorized use of this publication to train generative artificial intelligence (AI) technologies is expressly prohibited. HarperCollins also exercises their rights under Article 4(3) of the Digital Single Market Directive 2019/790 and expressly reserves this publication from the text and data mining exception.
harpercollins.com

Library of Congress Cataloging-in-Publication Data
Names: Tabor, Corey R. author | Webb, Dalton illustrator
Title: Hide-and-seek / story by Corey R. Tabor ; pictures by Dalton Webb.
Description: First edition. | New York : Greenwillow Books, an Imprint of HarperCollins Publishers, 2026. | Series: Wally mammoth ; book 2 | Audience: Ages 4-8 | Audience: Grades K-1 |
Summary: "When good friends in the Ice Age play a game of hide-and-seek, Wolf is aided by his snow-white fur that blends in with the arctic landscape"— Provided by publisher.
Identifiers: LCCN 2025013595 | ISBN 9780063434943 hardcover
Subjects: CYAC: Woolly mammoth—Fiction | Mammoths—Fiction | Prehistoric animals—Fiction | Hide-and-seek—Fiction | LCGFT: Animal fiction | Picture books
Classification: LCC PZ7.1.T29 Wal 2026 | DDC [E] —dc23/eng/20250723
LC record available at https://lccn.loc.gov/2025013595

The artwork for this book was created using digital watercolor
and pencil brushes in Procreate on an iPad.
The text of this book is set in 22-point ICRC. Book design by Paul Zakris.
25 26 27 28 29 RTLO 10 9 8 7 6 5 4 3 2 1
First Edition

Greenwillow Books

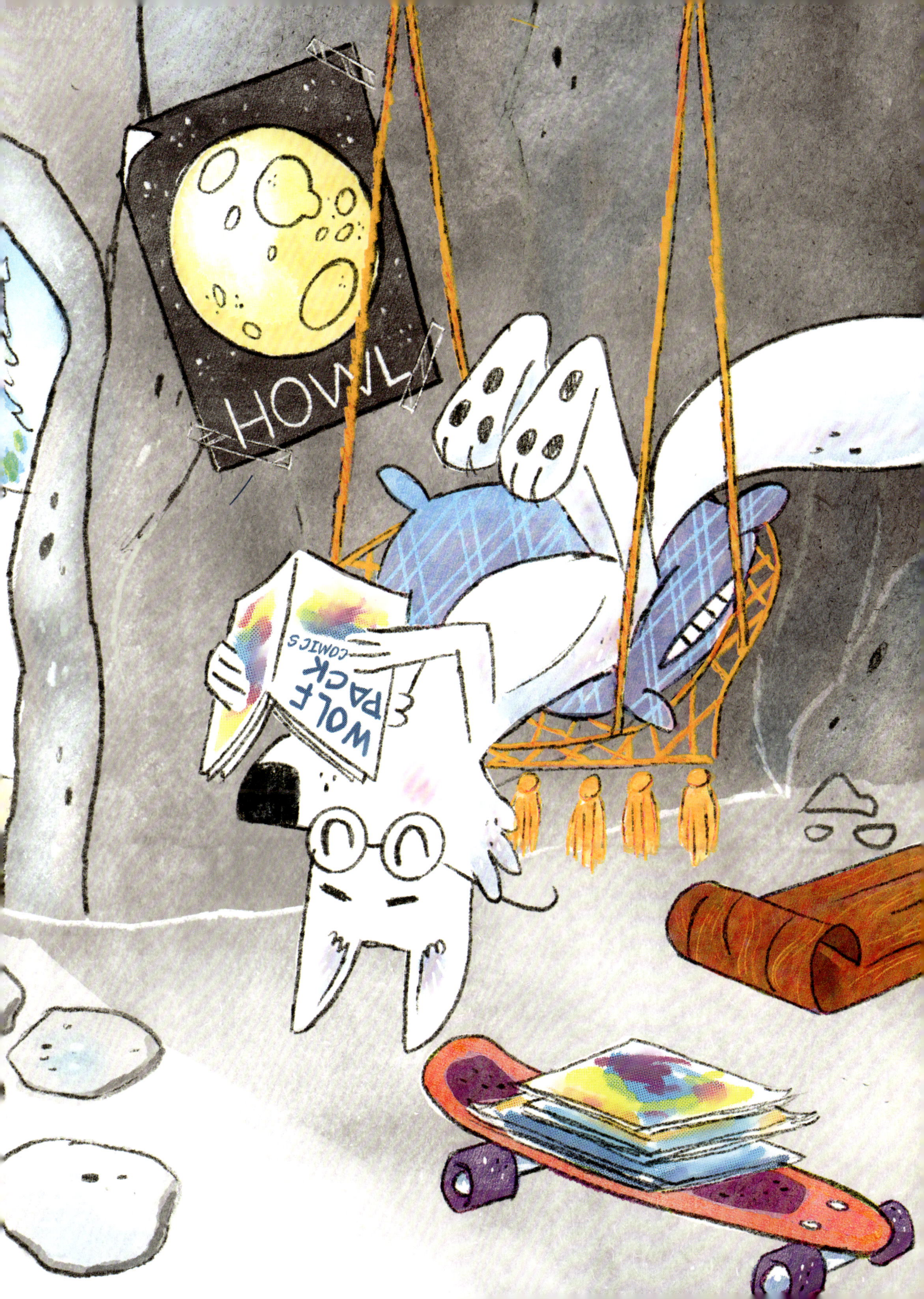
HOWL
WOLF PACK
COMICS

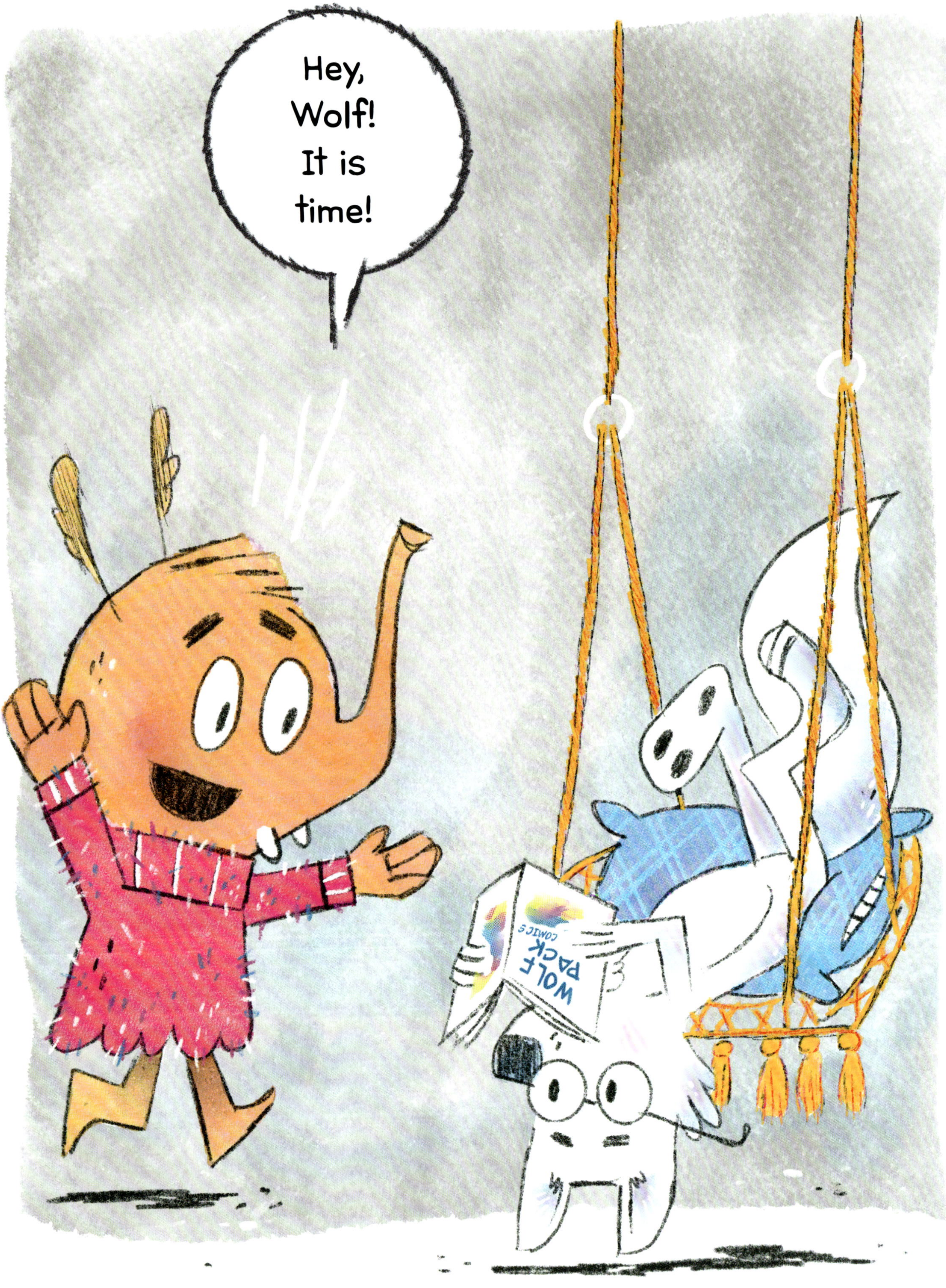
Hey, Wolf! It is time!
WOLF PACK
COMICS

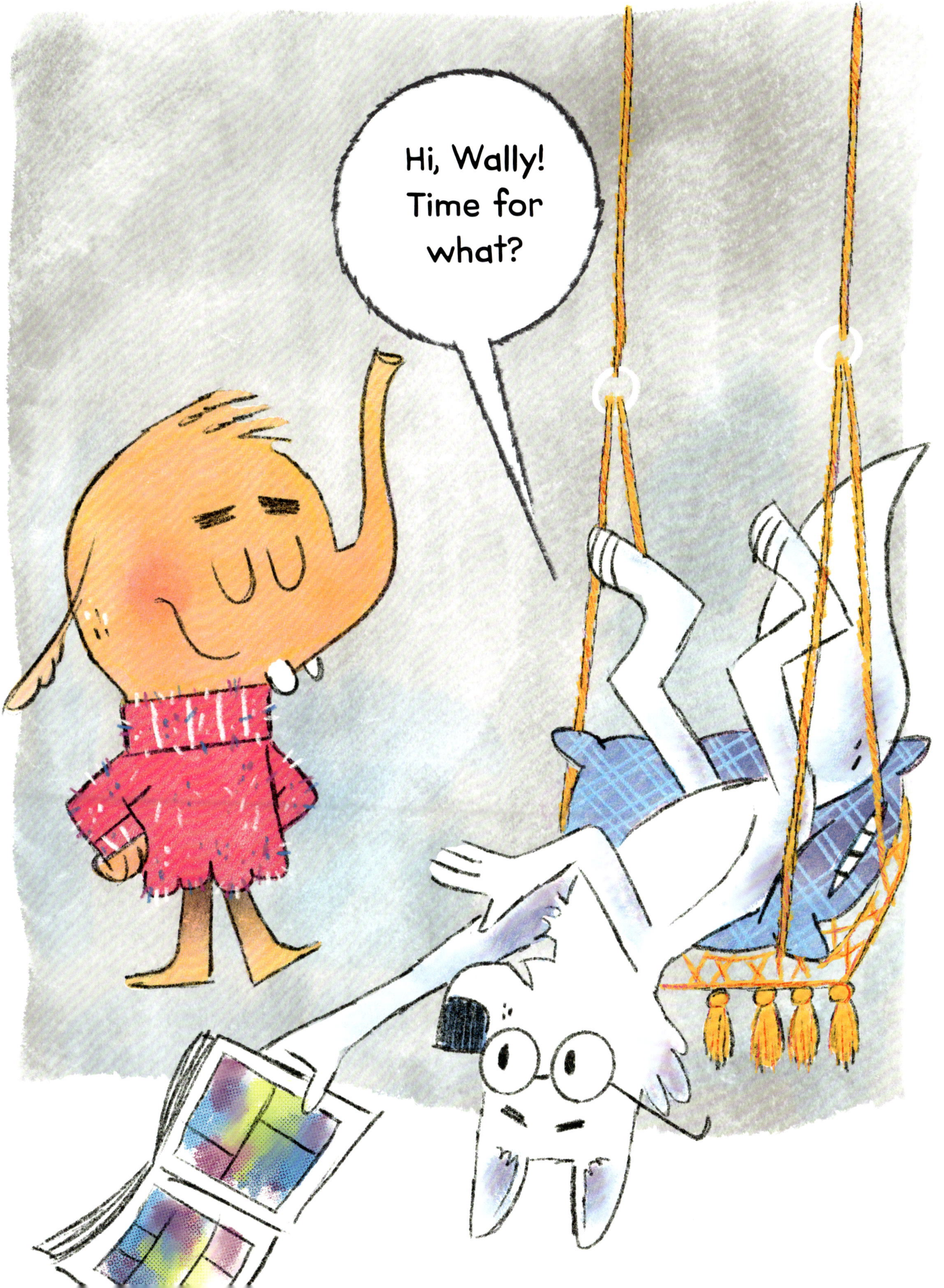
Hi, Wally! Time for what?

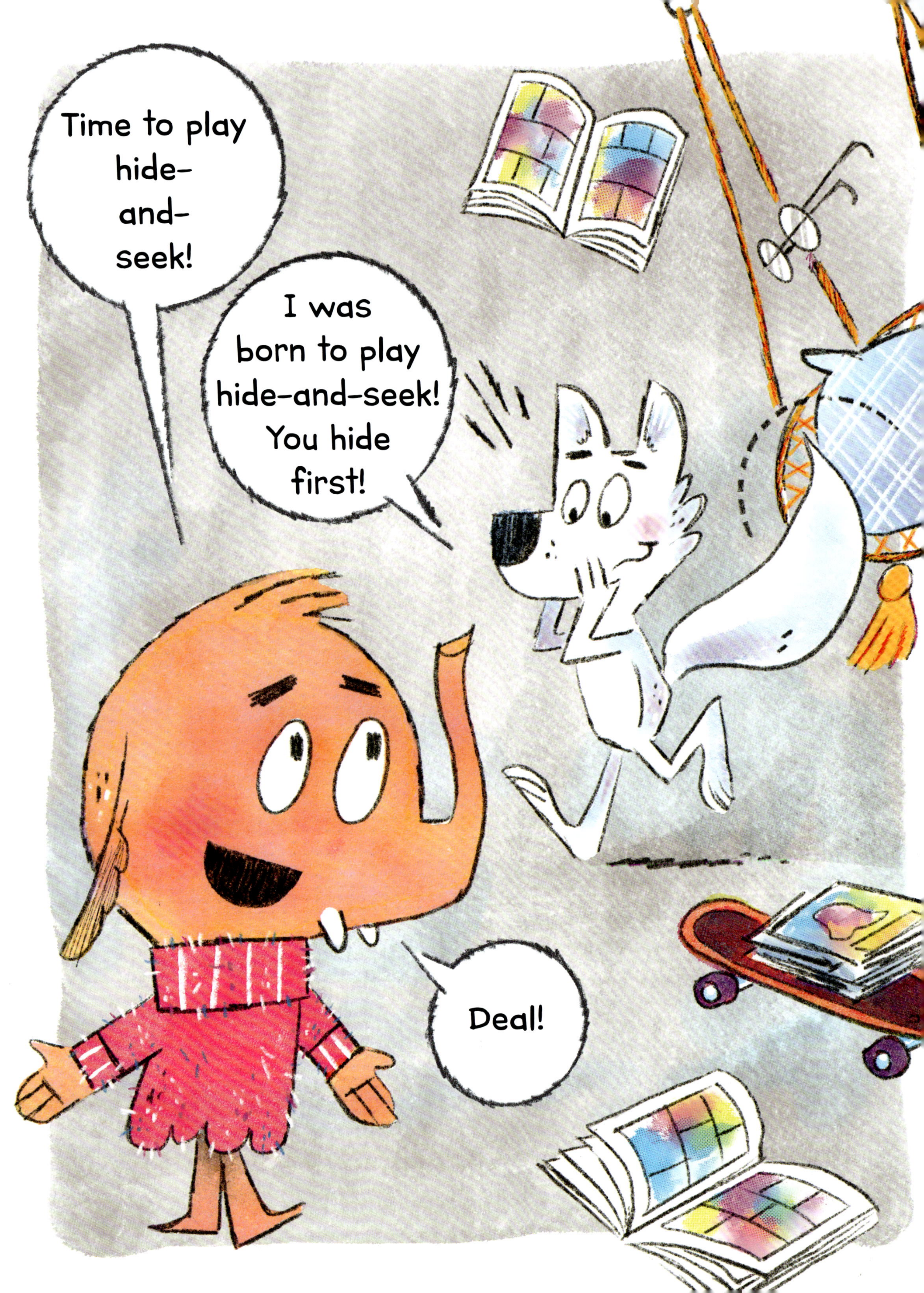
Time to play hide-and-seek!
I was born to play hide-and-seek! You hide first!
Deal!

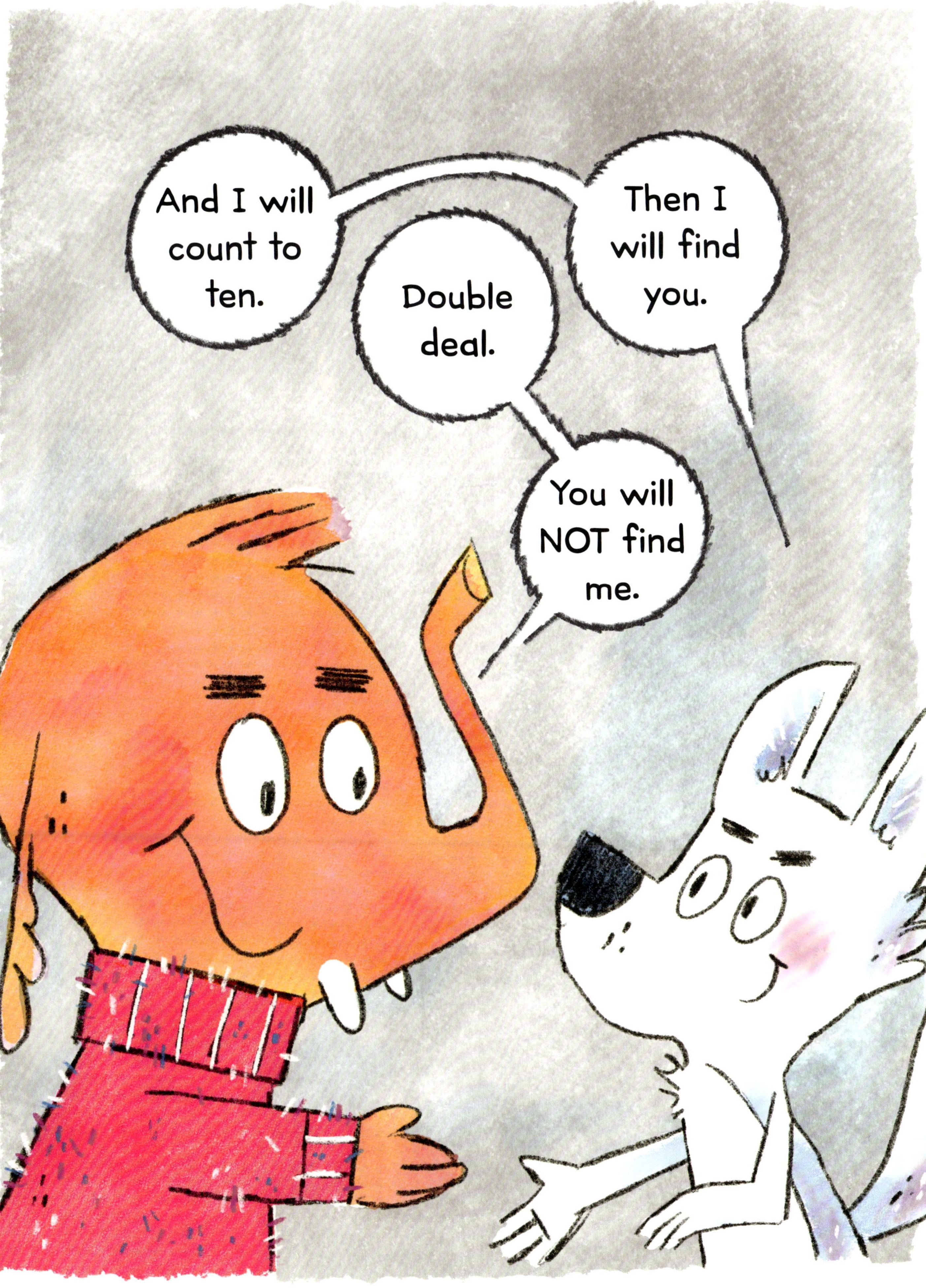
And I will count to ten.
Then I will find you.
Double deal.
You will NOT find me.

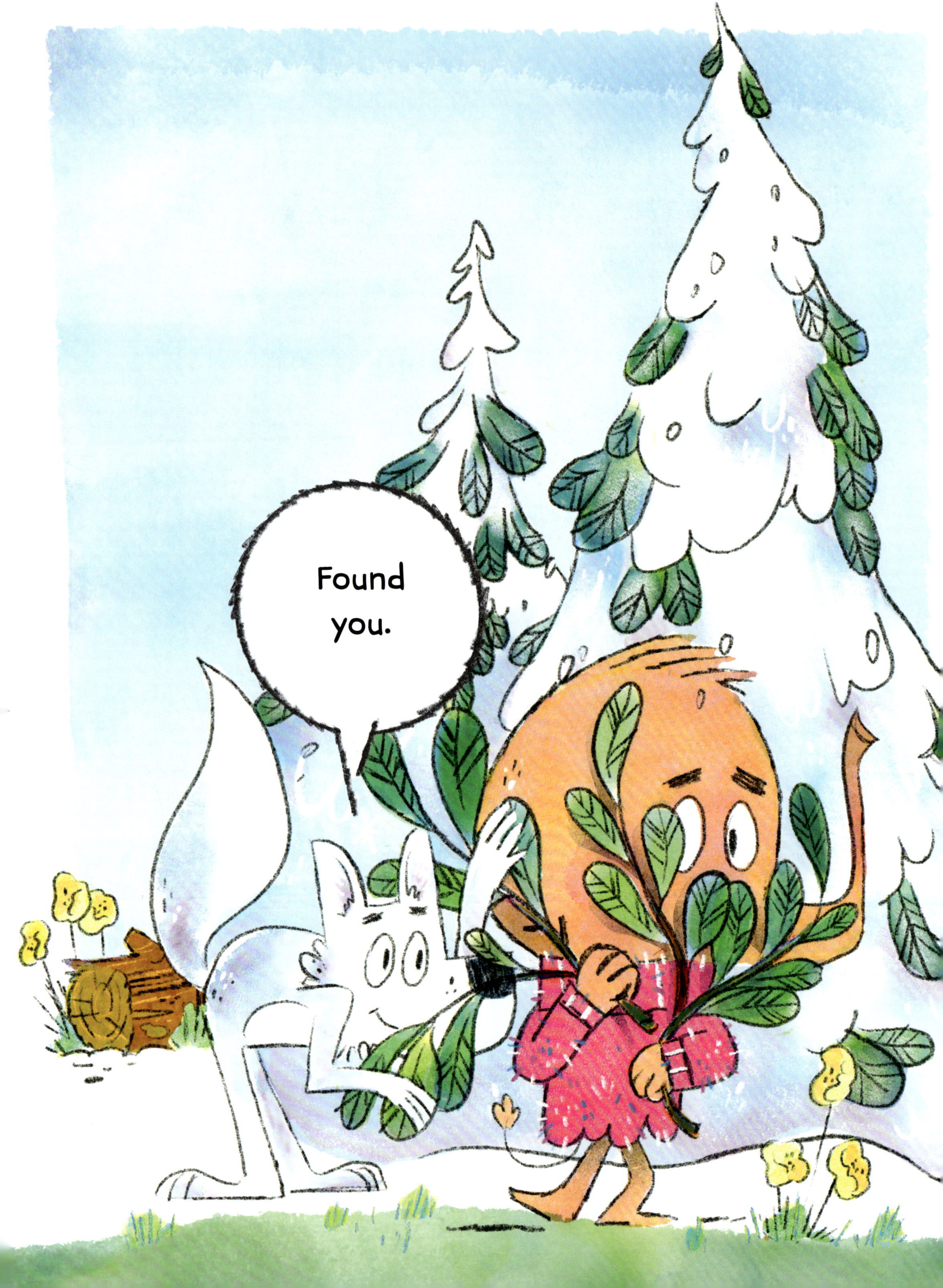
Found you.

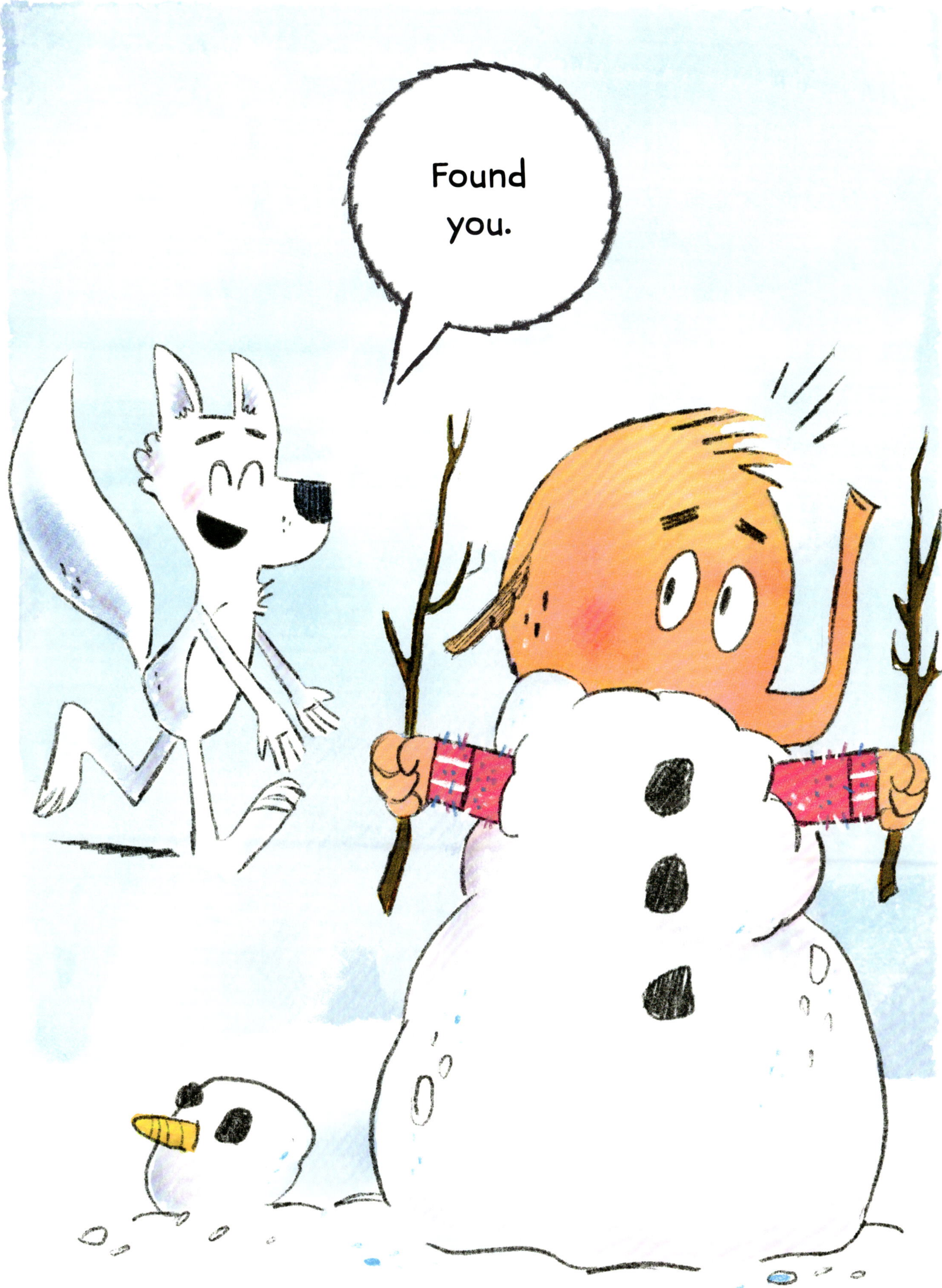
Found you.

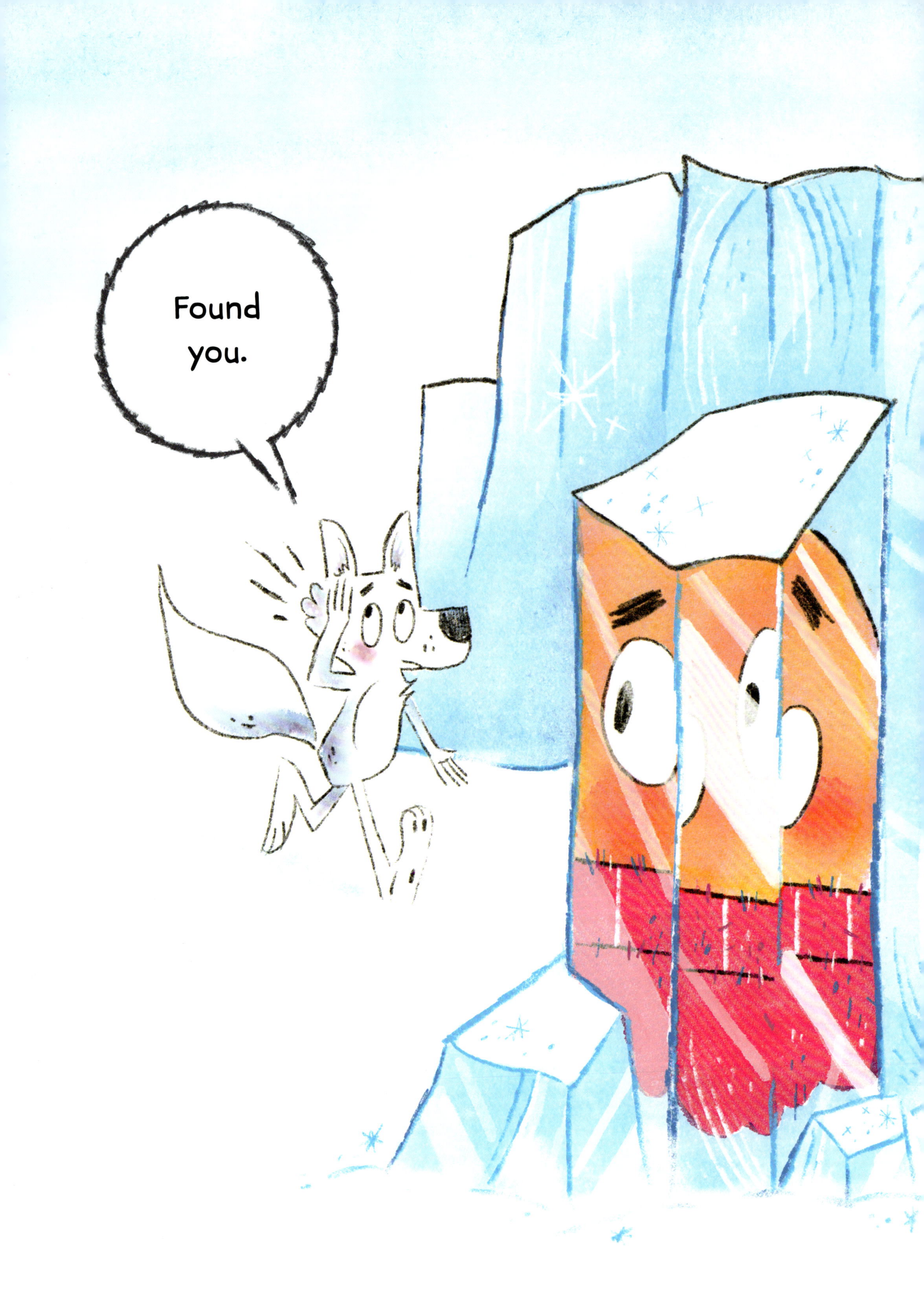
Found you.

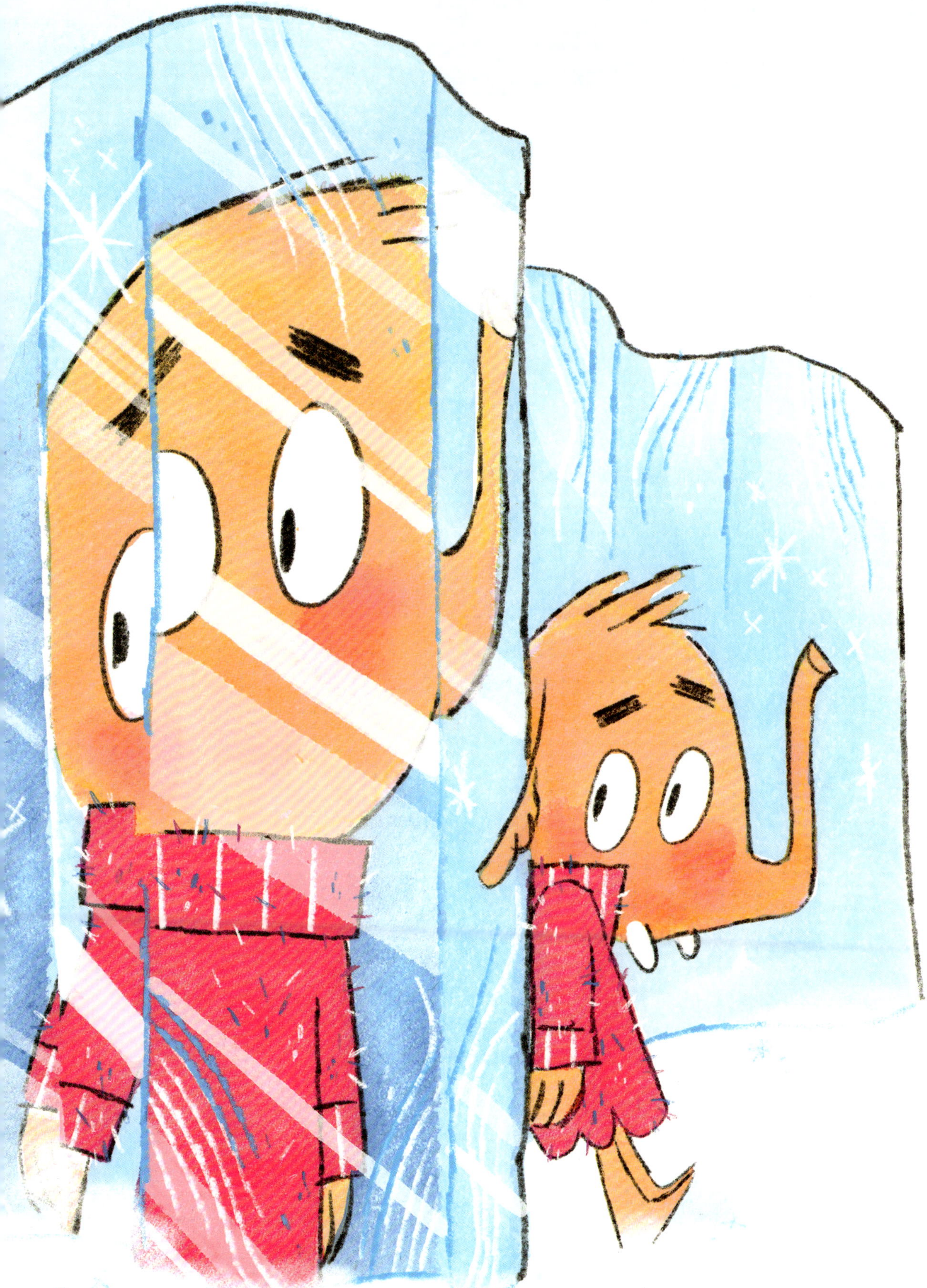

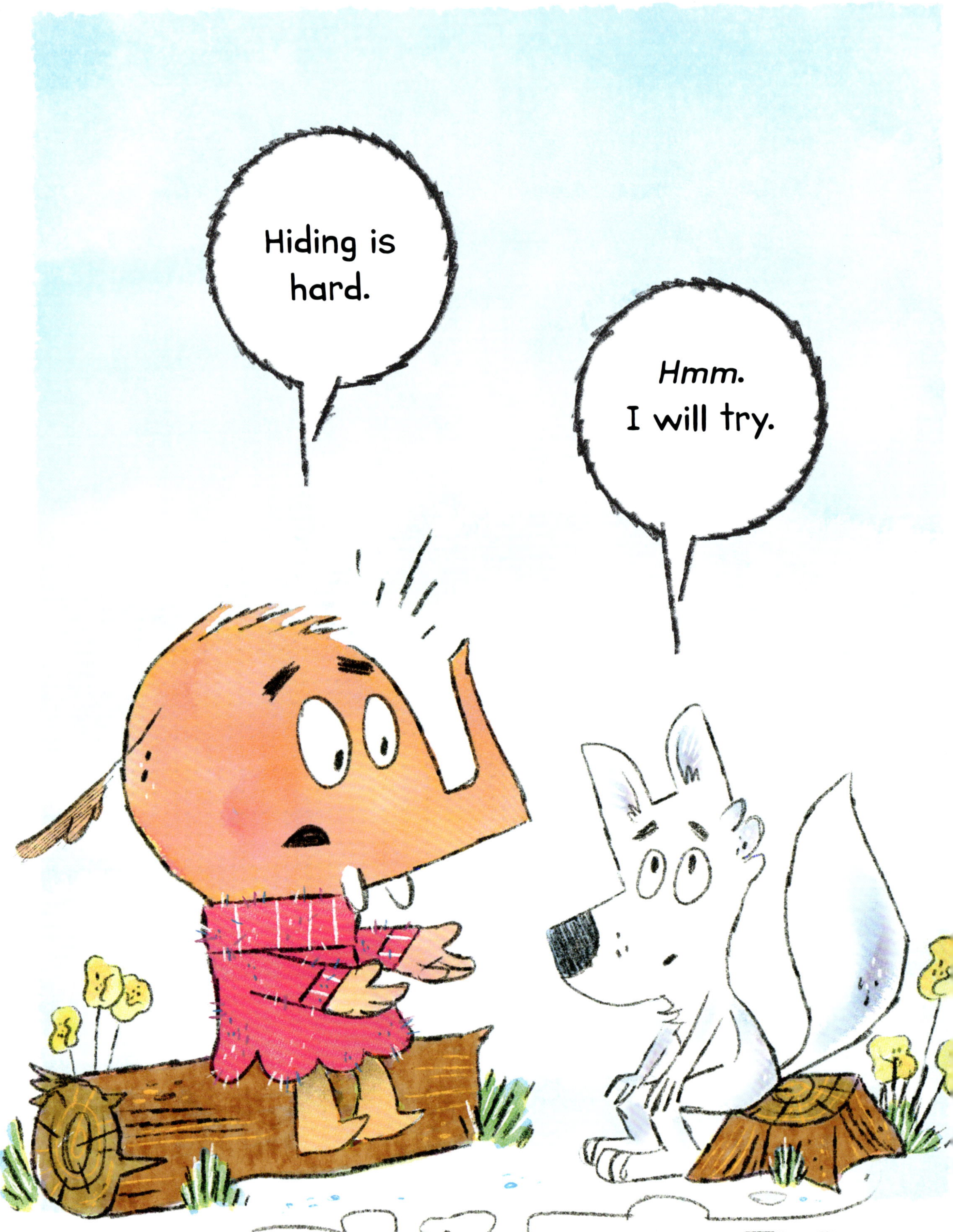
Hiding is hard.
Hmm. I will try.

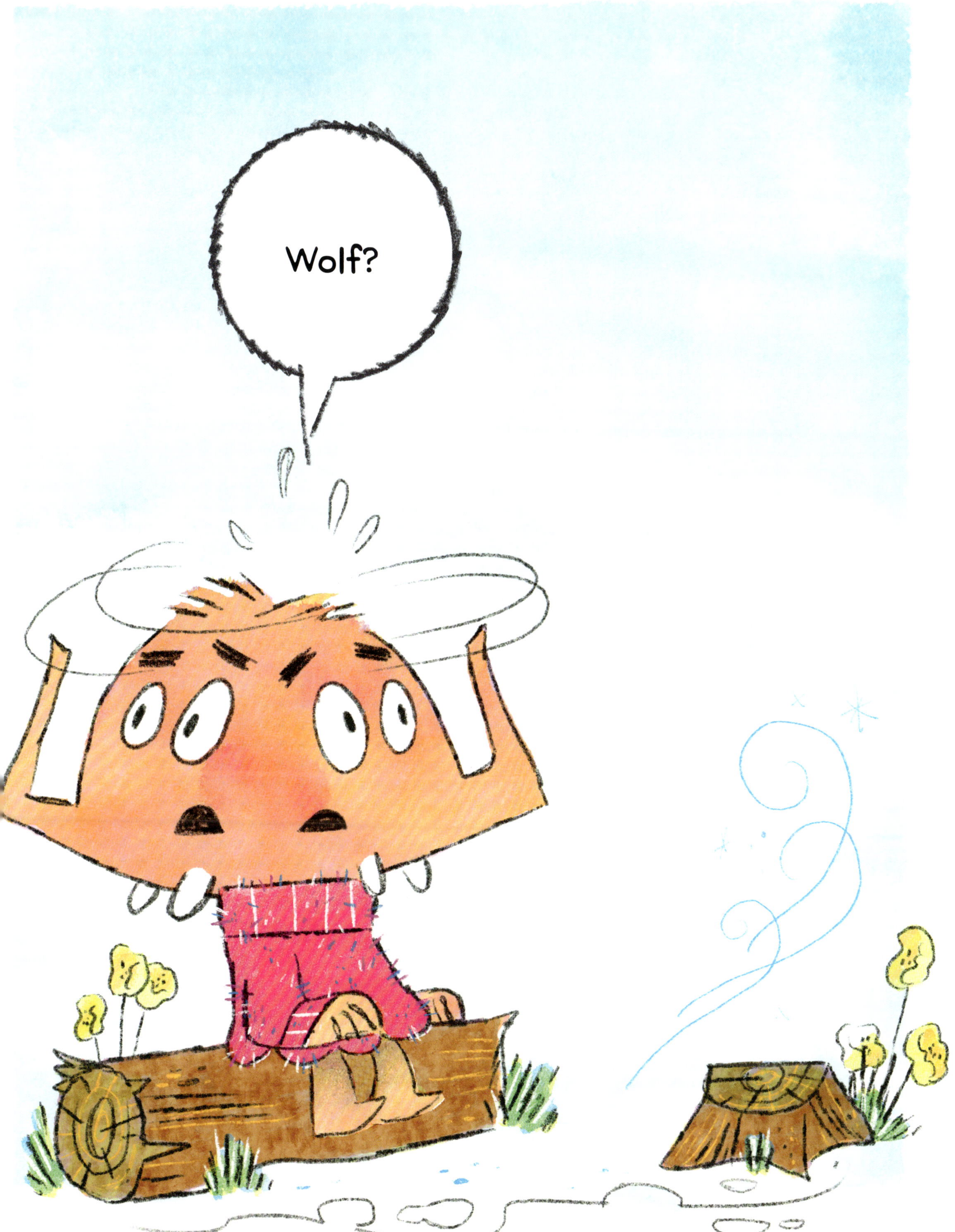
Wolf?

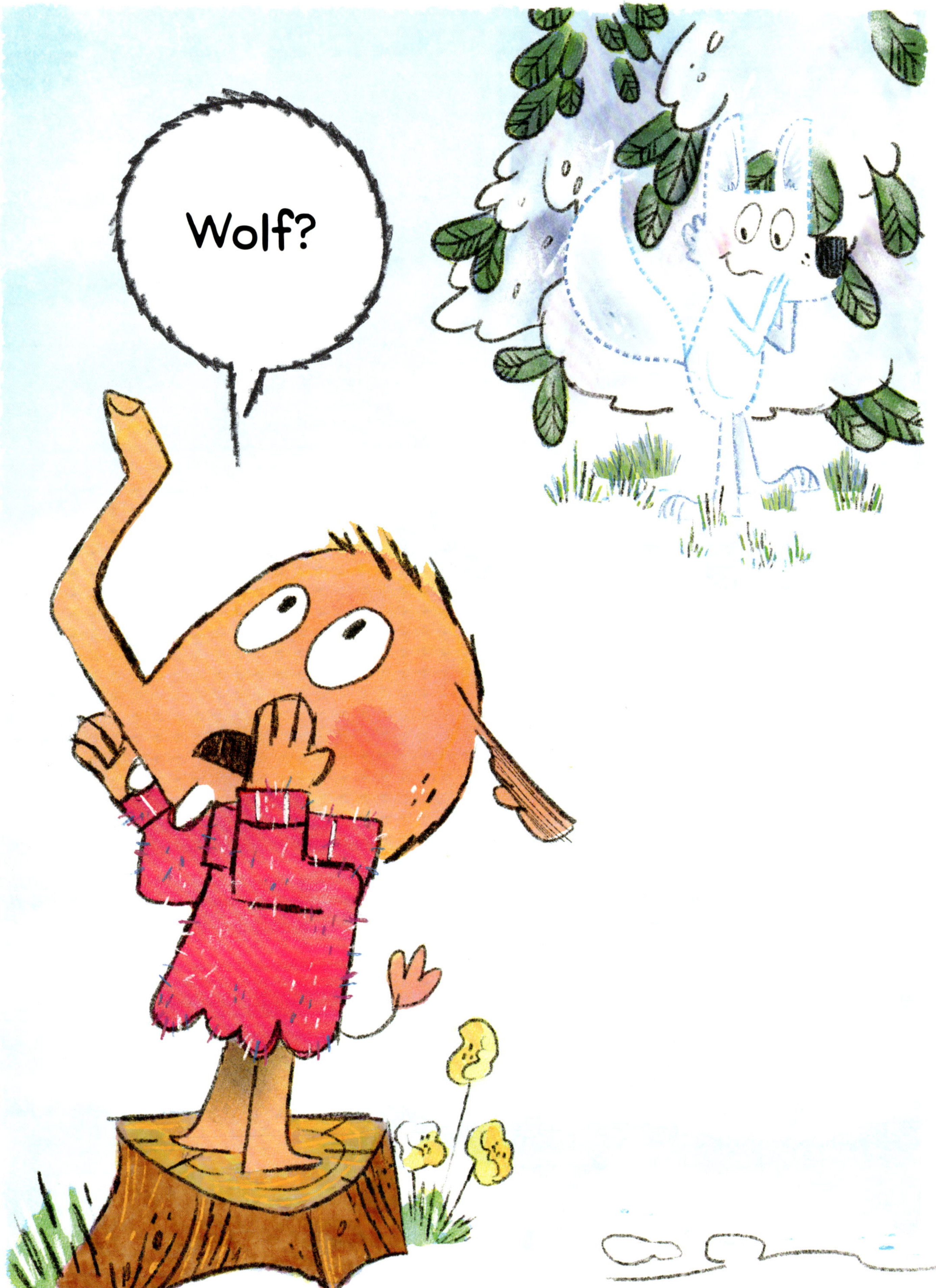
Wolf?

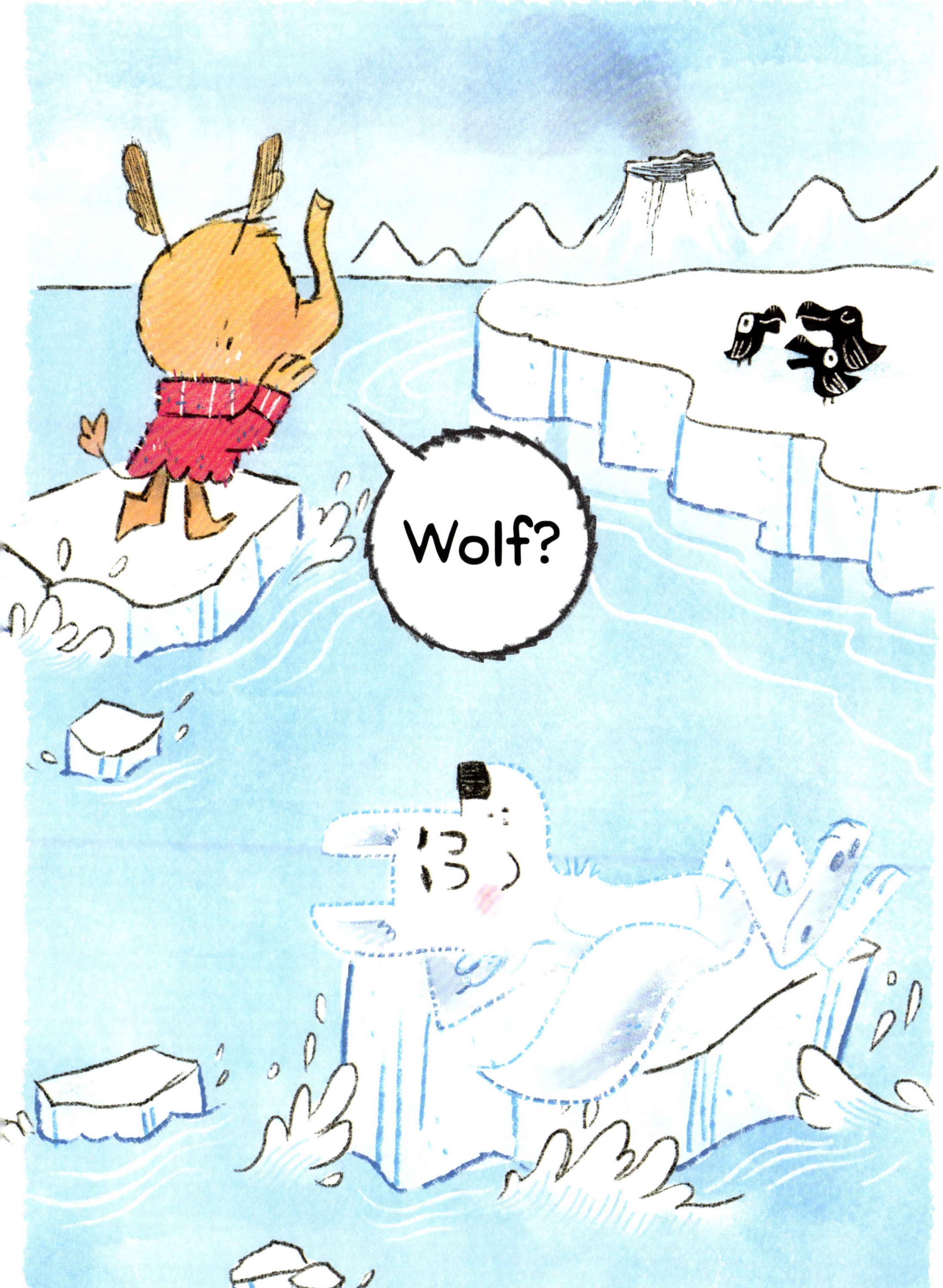
Wolf?

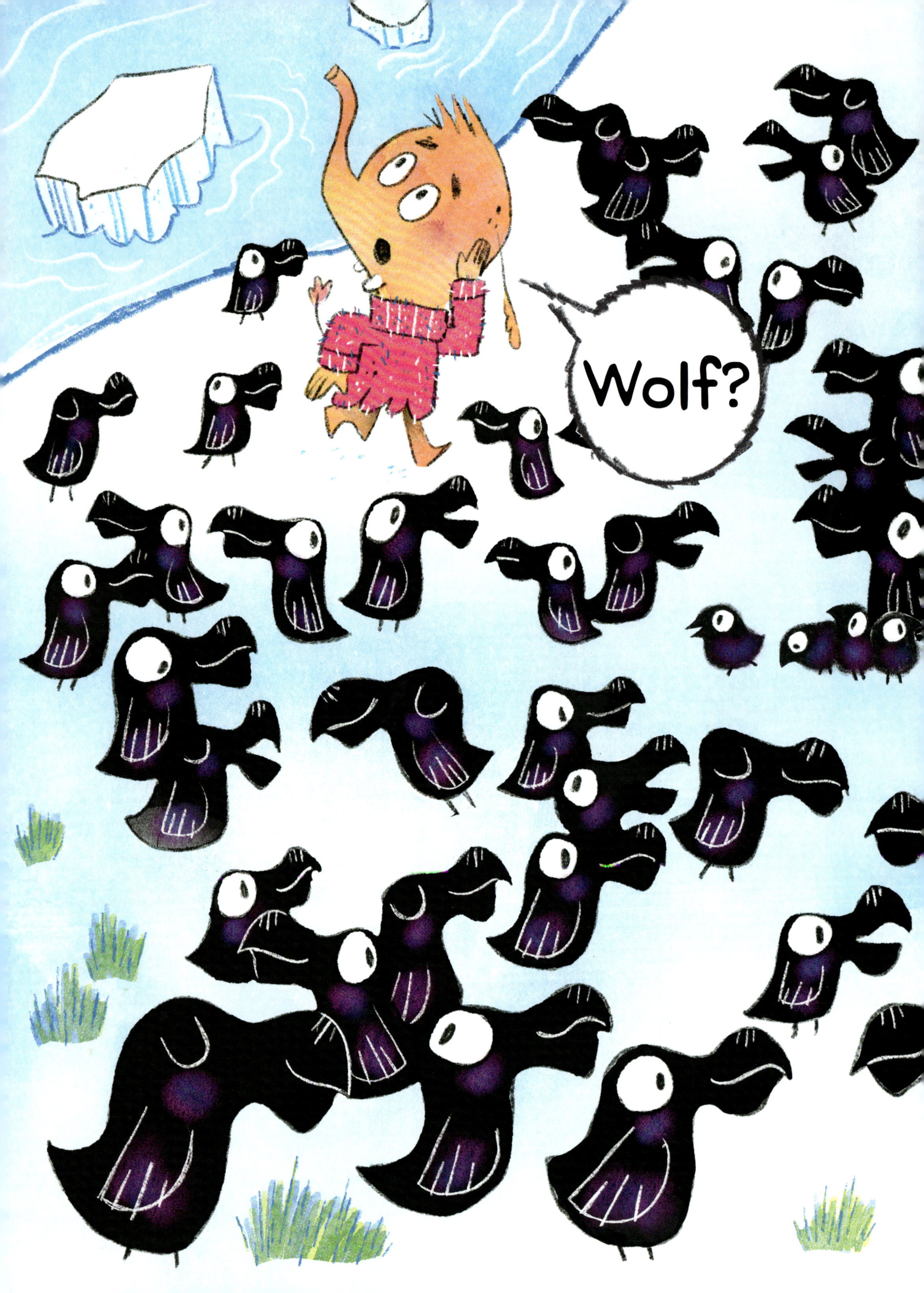
Wolf?

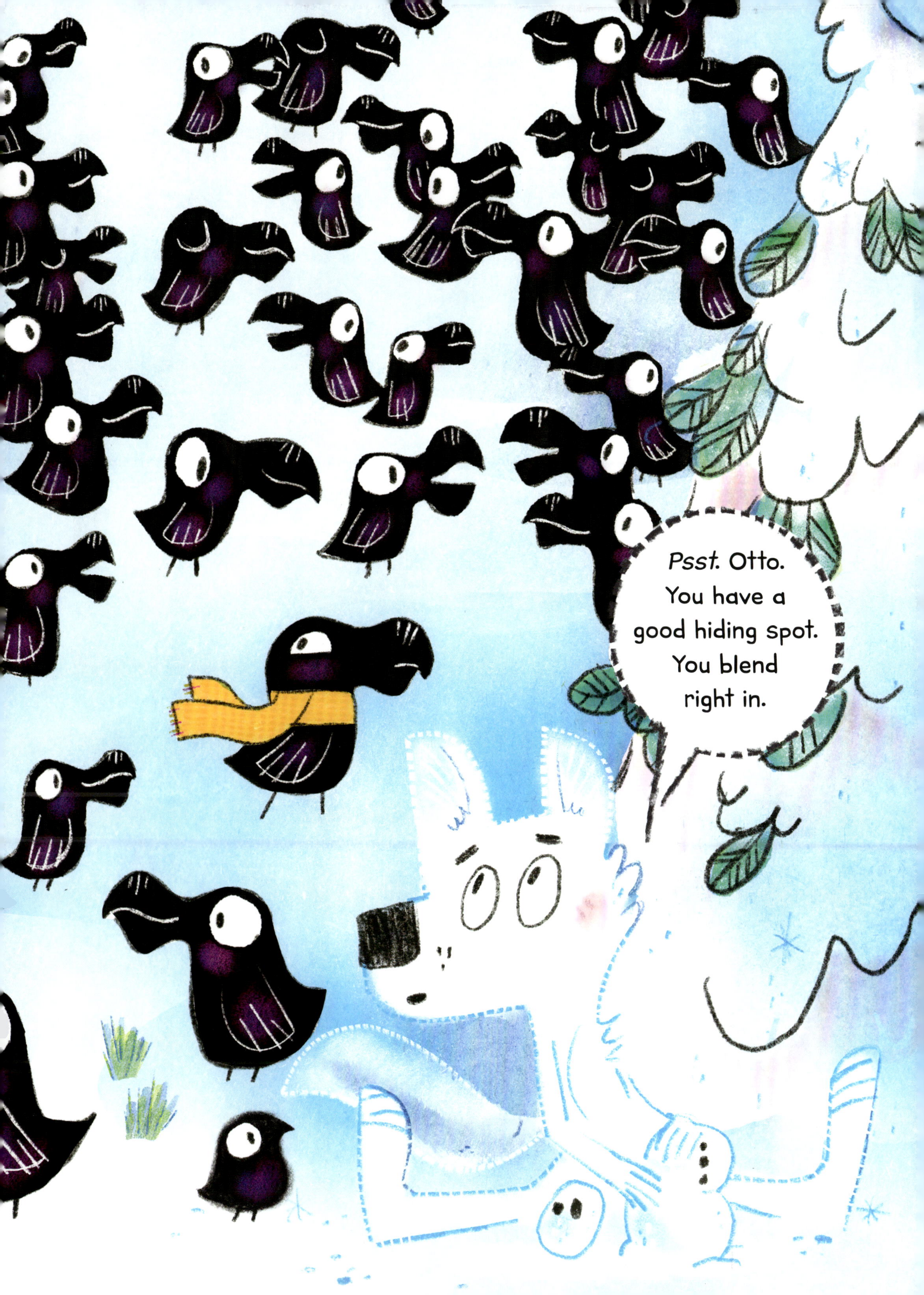
Psst. Otto. You have a good hiding spot. You blend right in.

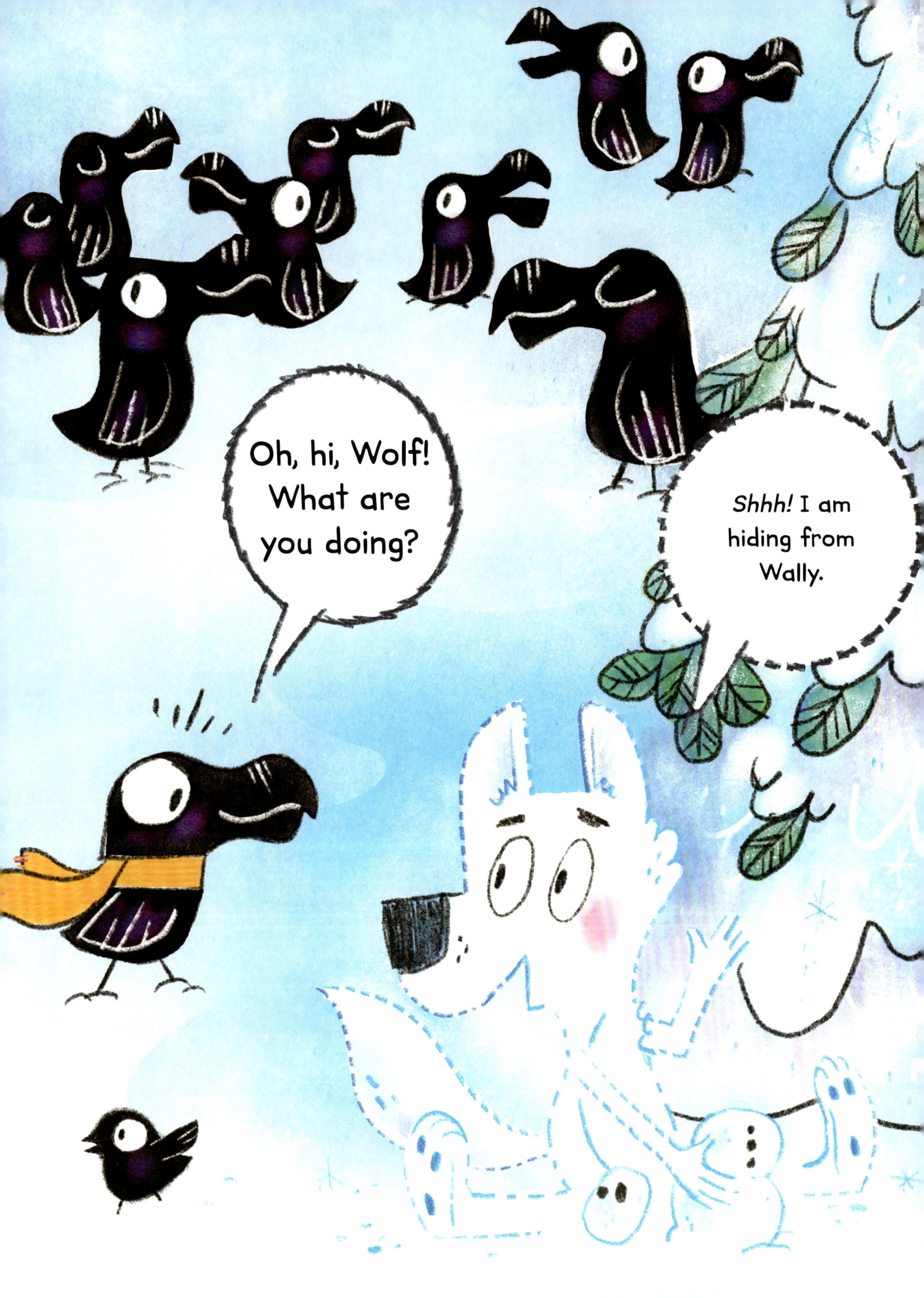
Oh, hi, Wolf! What are you doing?
Shhh! I am hiding from Wally.

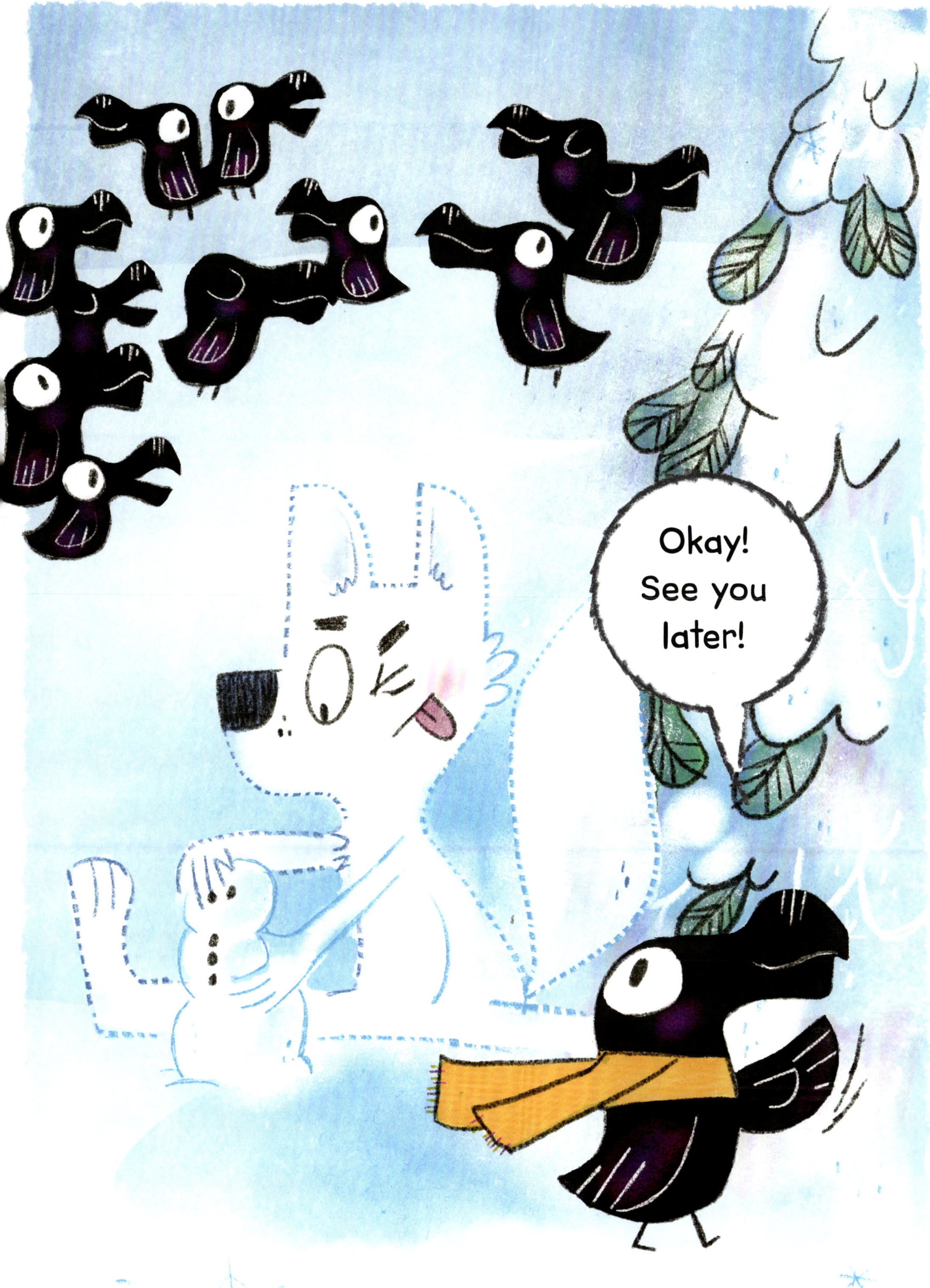
Okay! See you later!

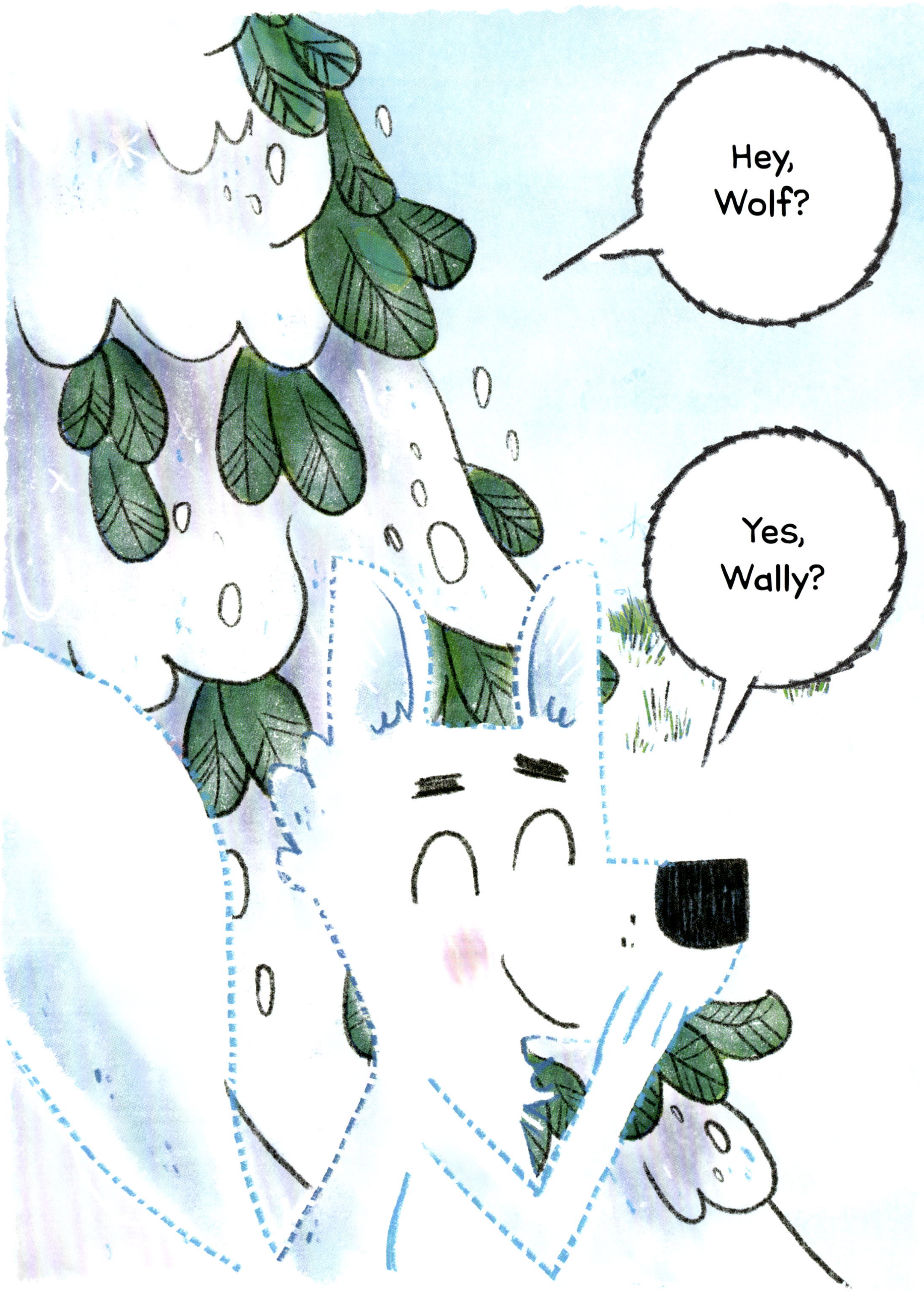
Hey, Wolf?
Yes, Wally?

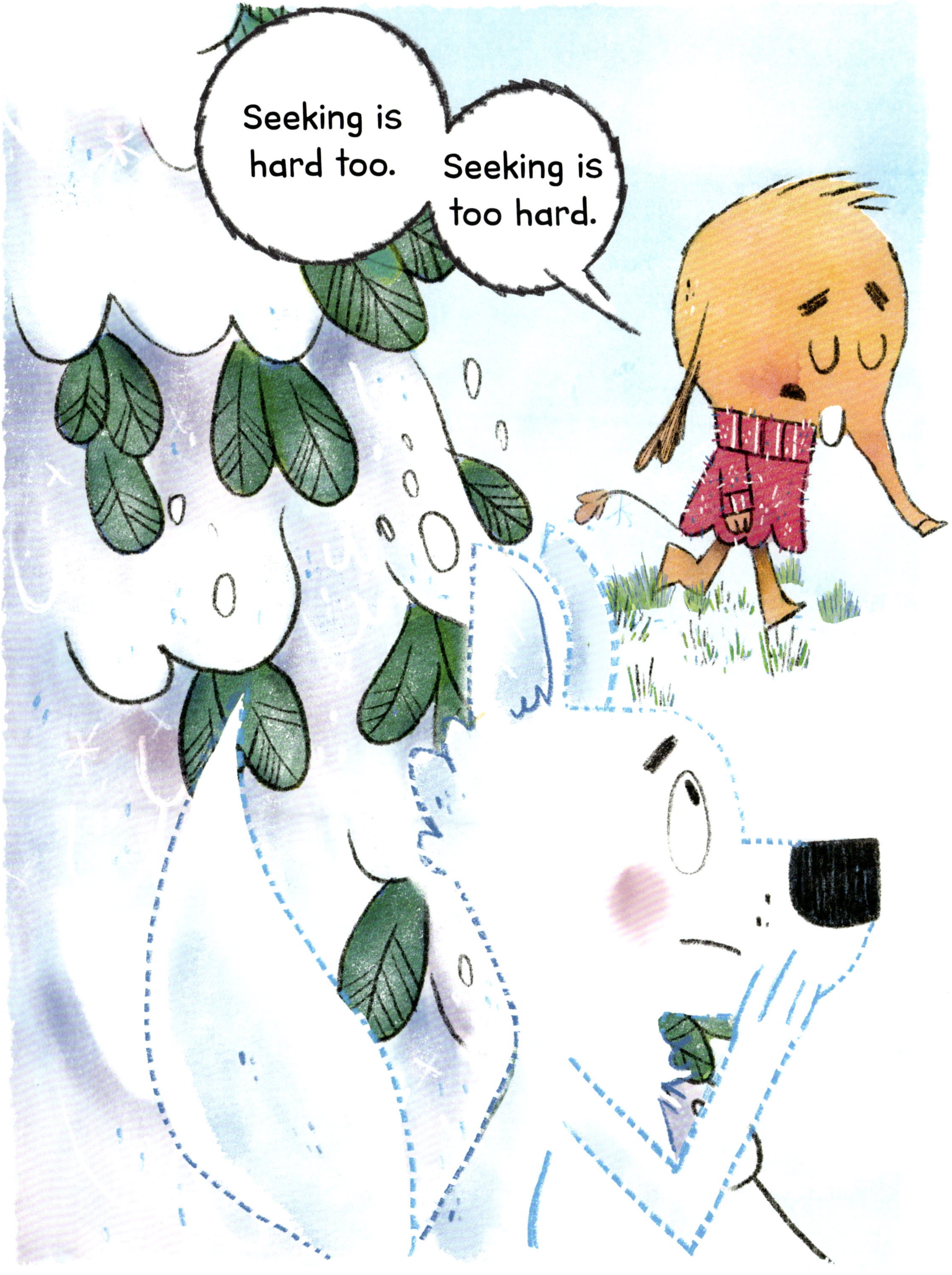
Seeking is hard too.
Seeking is too hard.

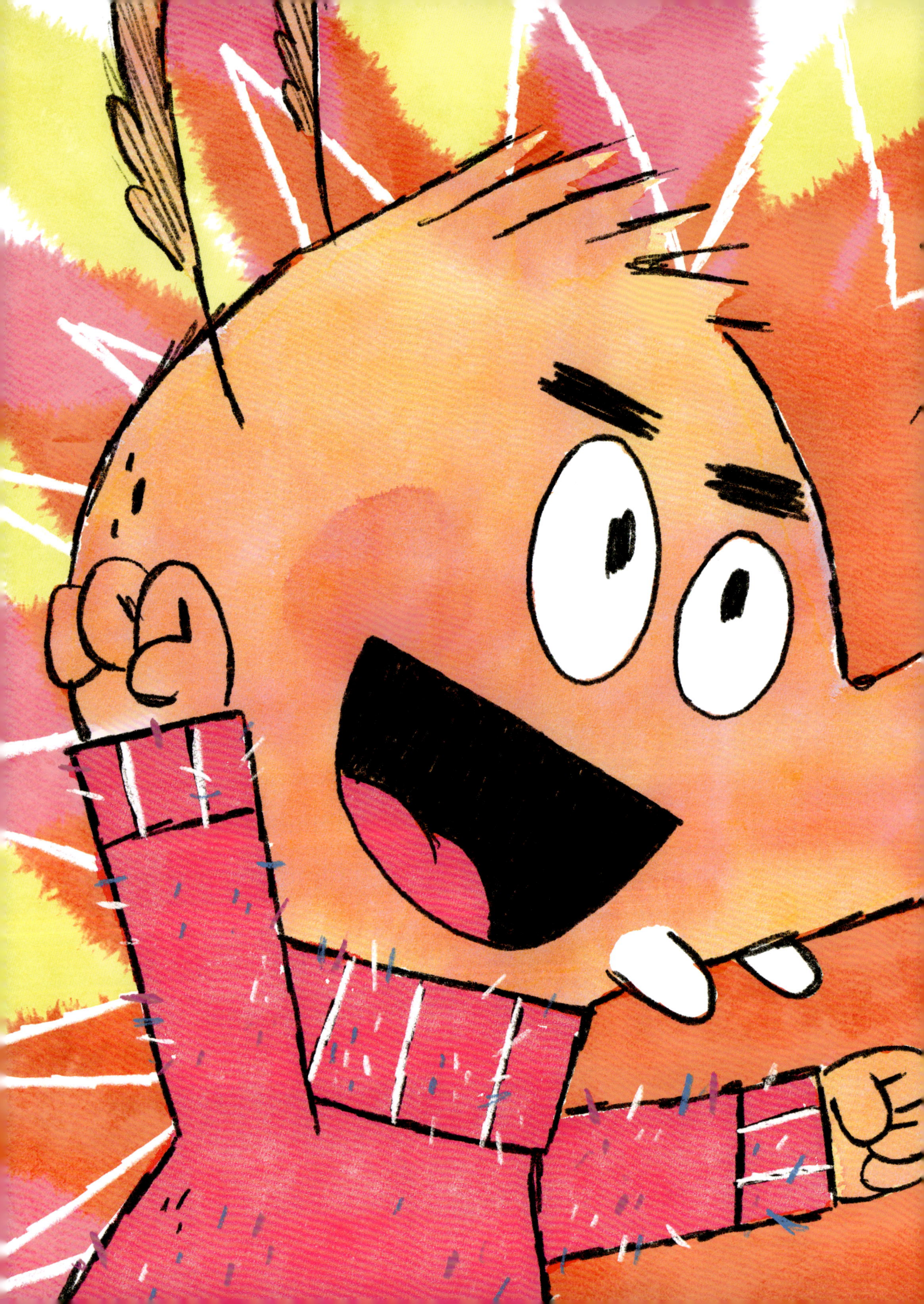

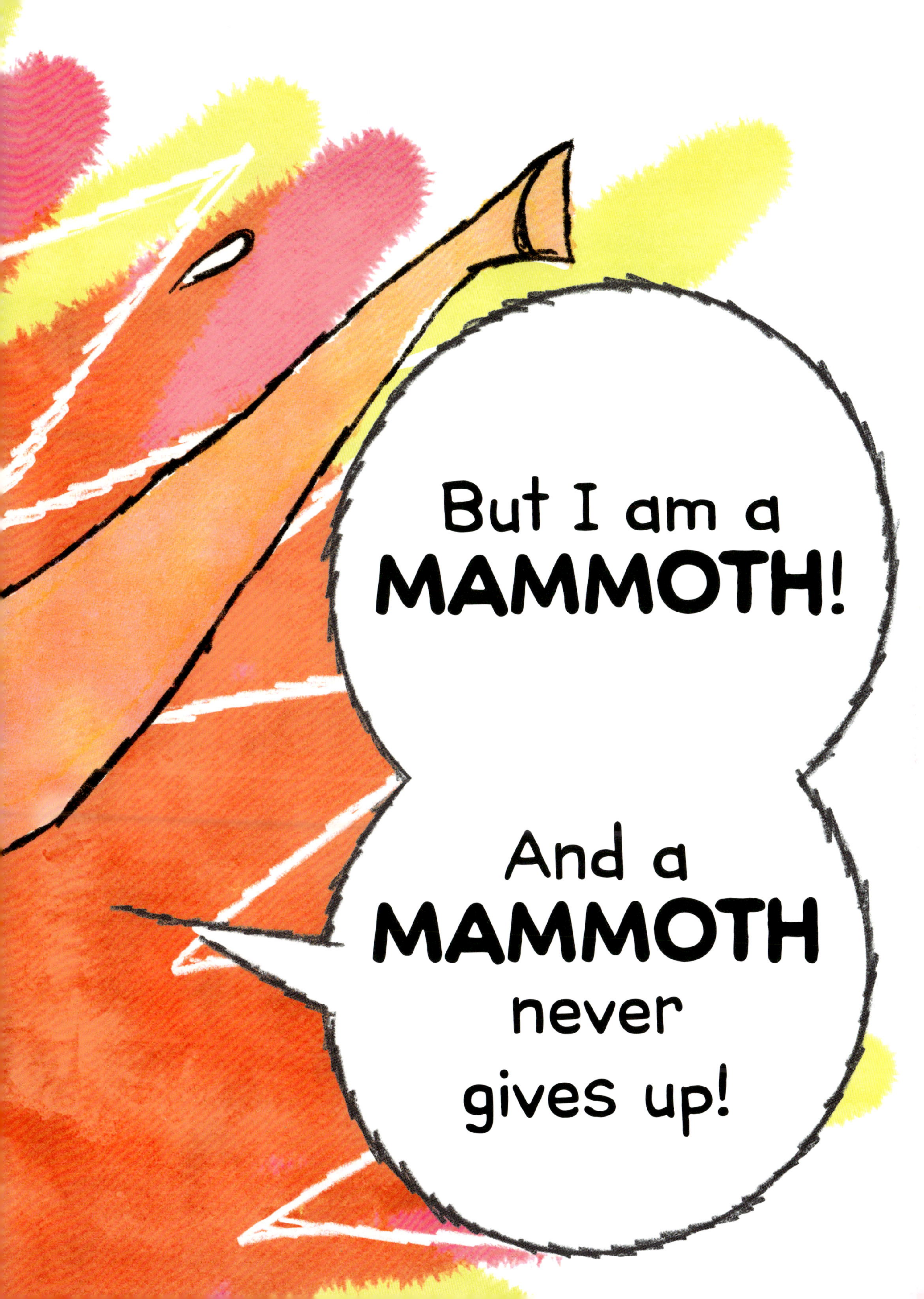
But I am a MAMMOTH!
And a MAMMOTH never gives up!

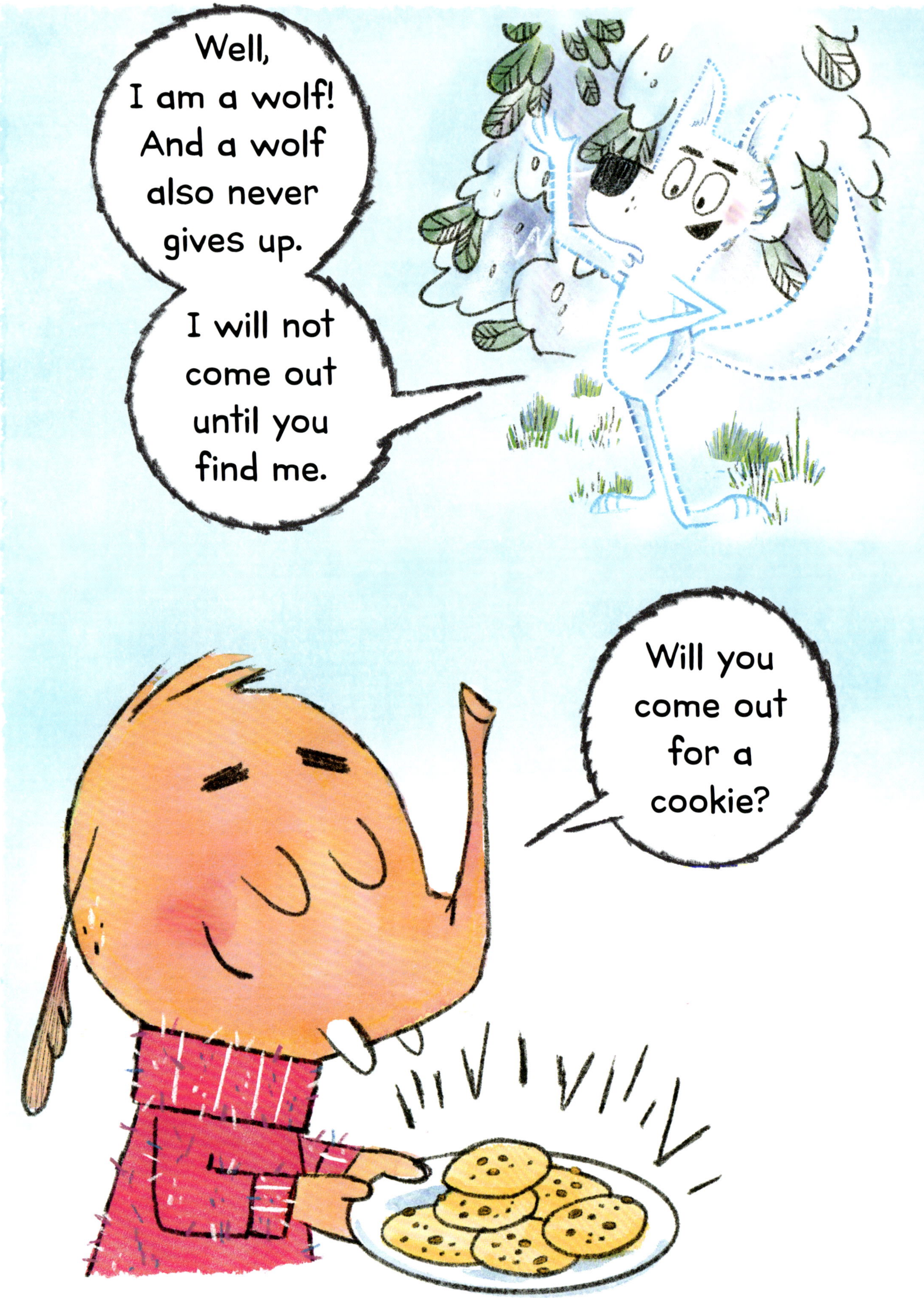
Well, I am a wolf! And a wolf also never gives up.
I will not come out until you find me.
Will you come out for a cookie?

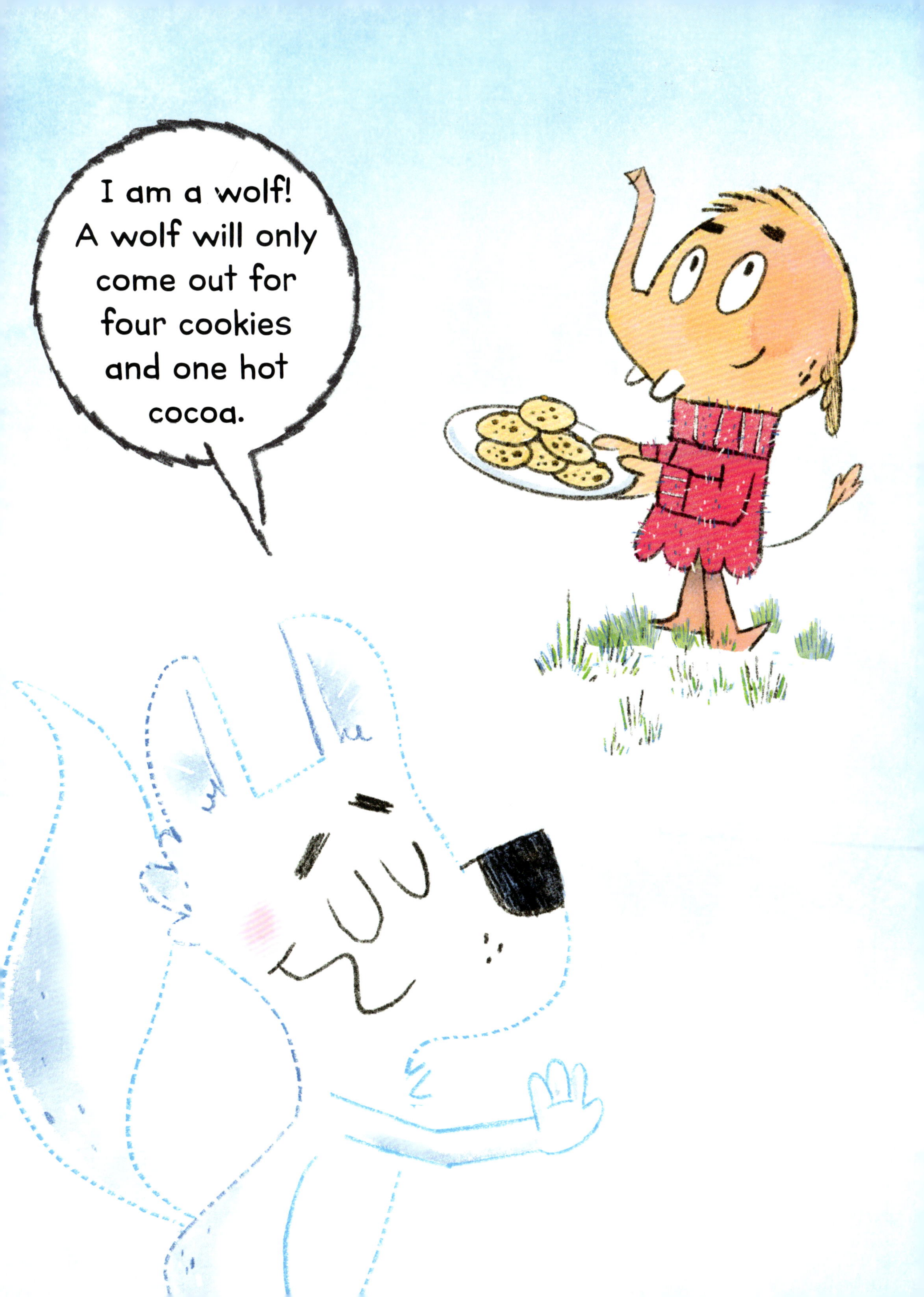
I am a wolf! A wolf will only come out for four cookies and one hot cocoa.

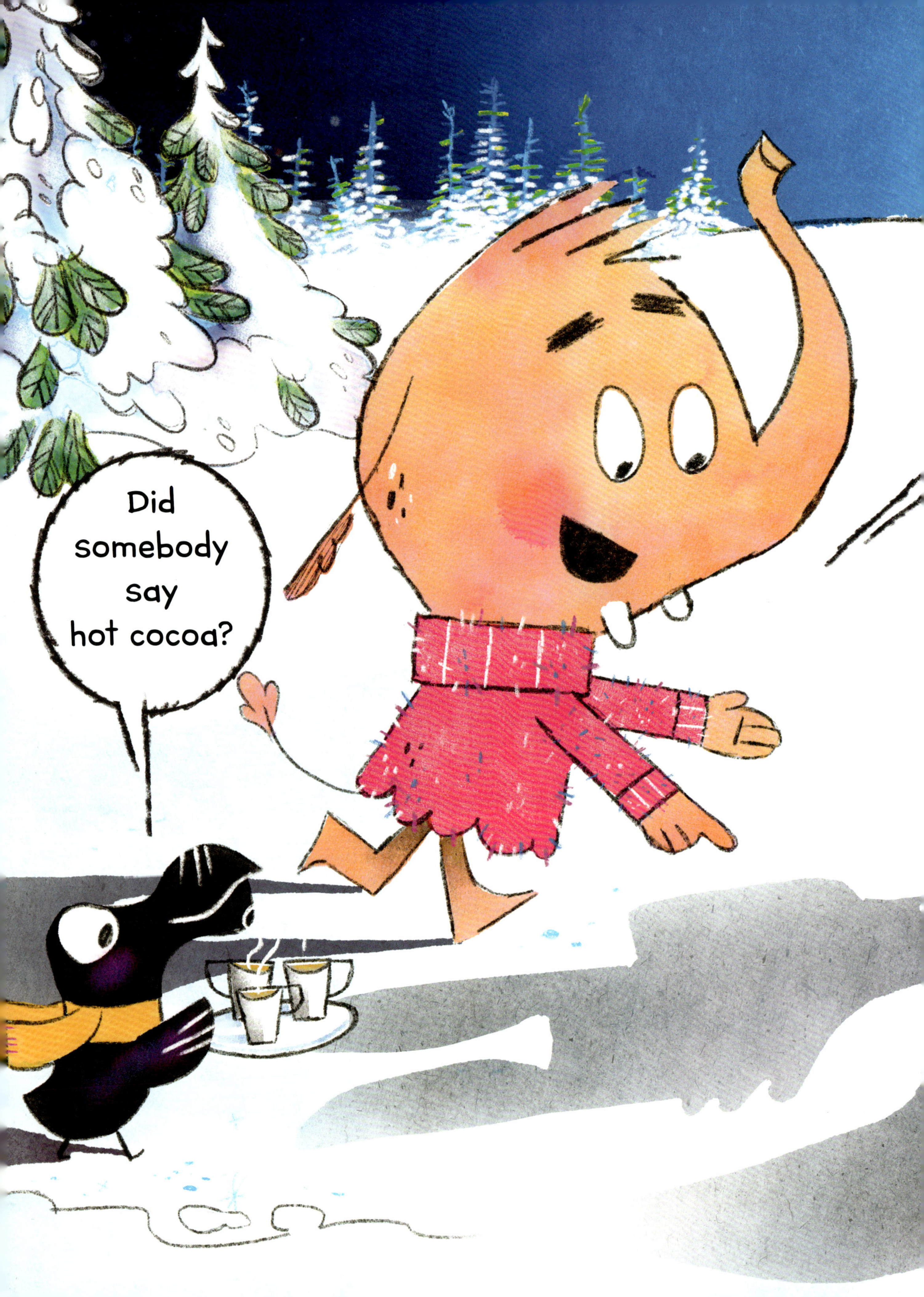
Did somebody say hot cocoa?

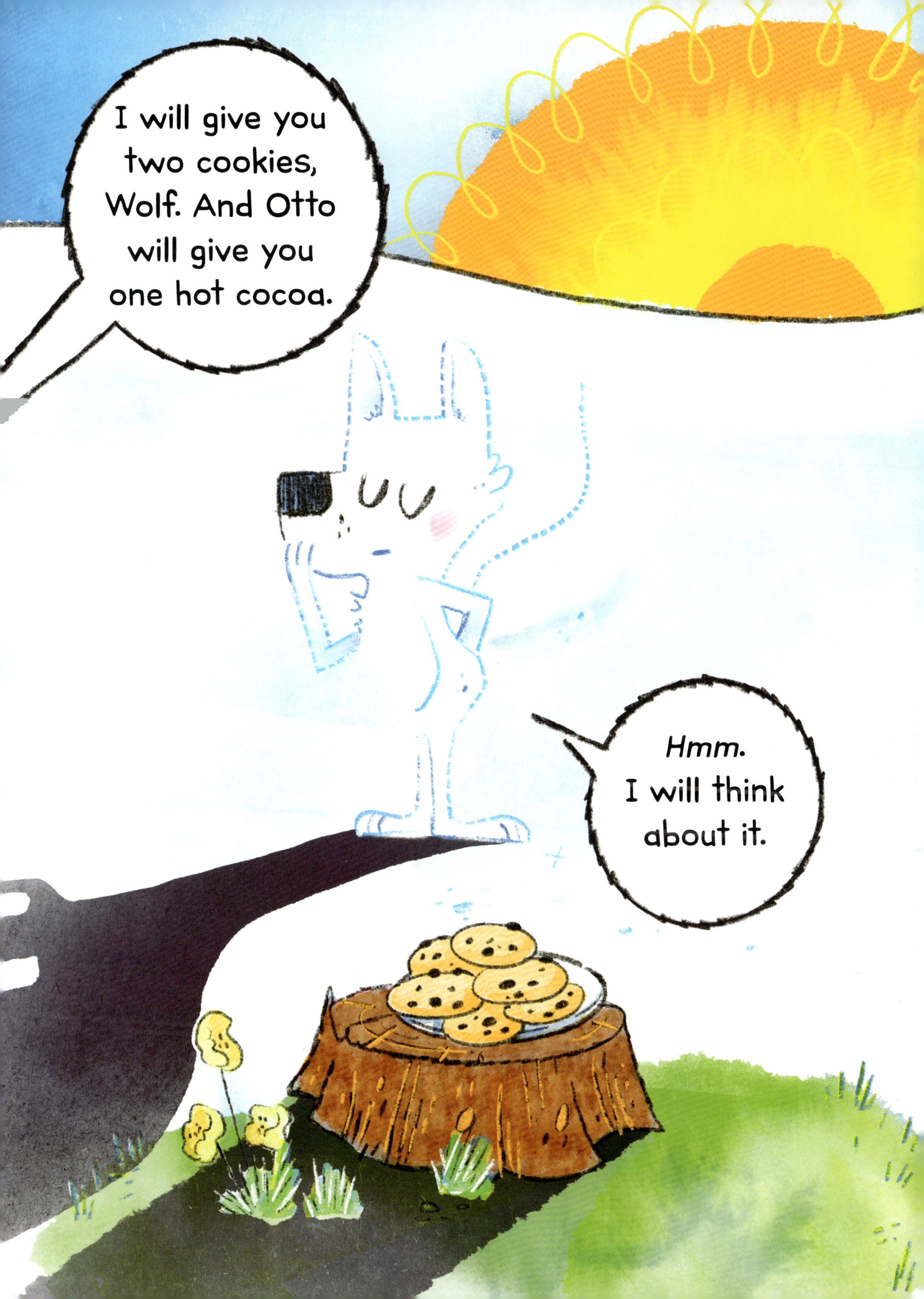
I will give you two cookies, Wolf. And Otto will give you one hot cocoa.
Hmm. I will think about it.

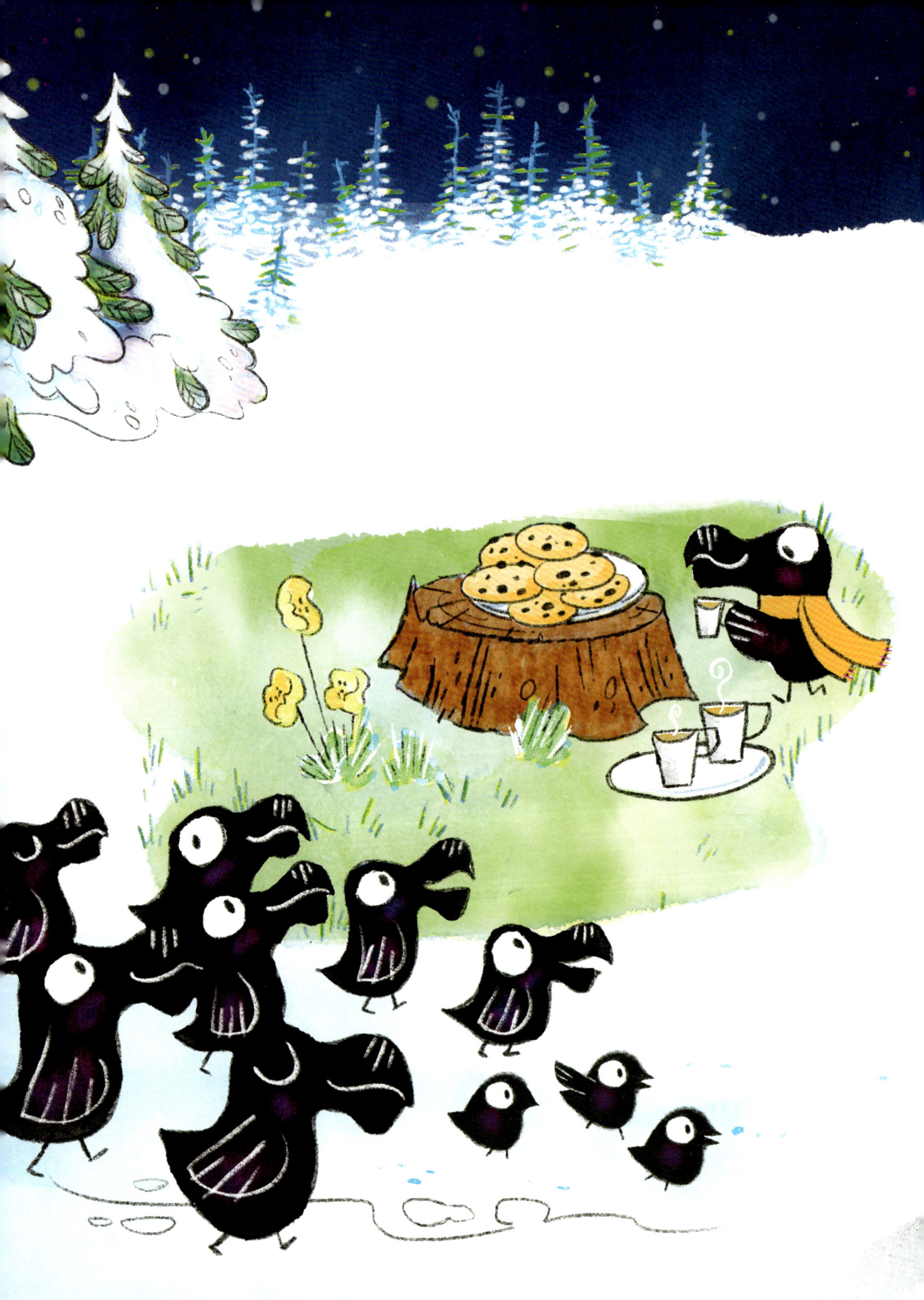

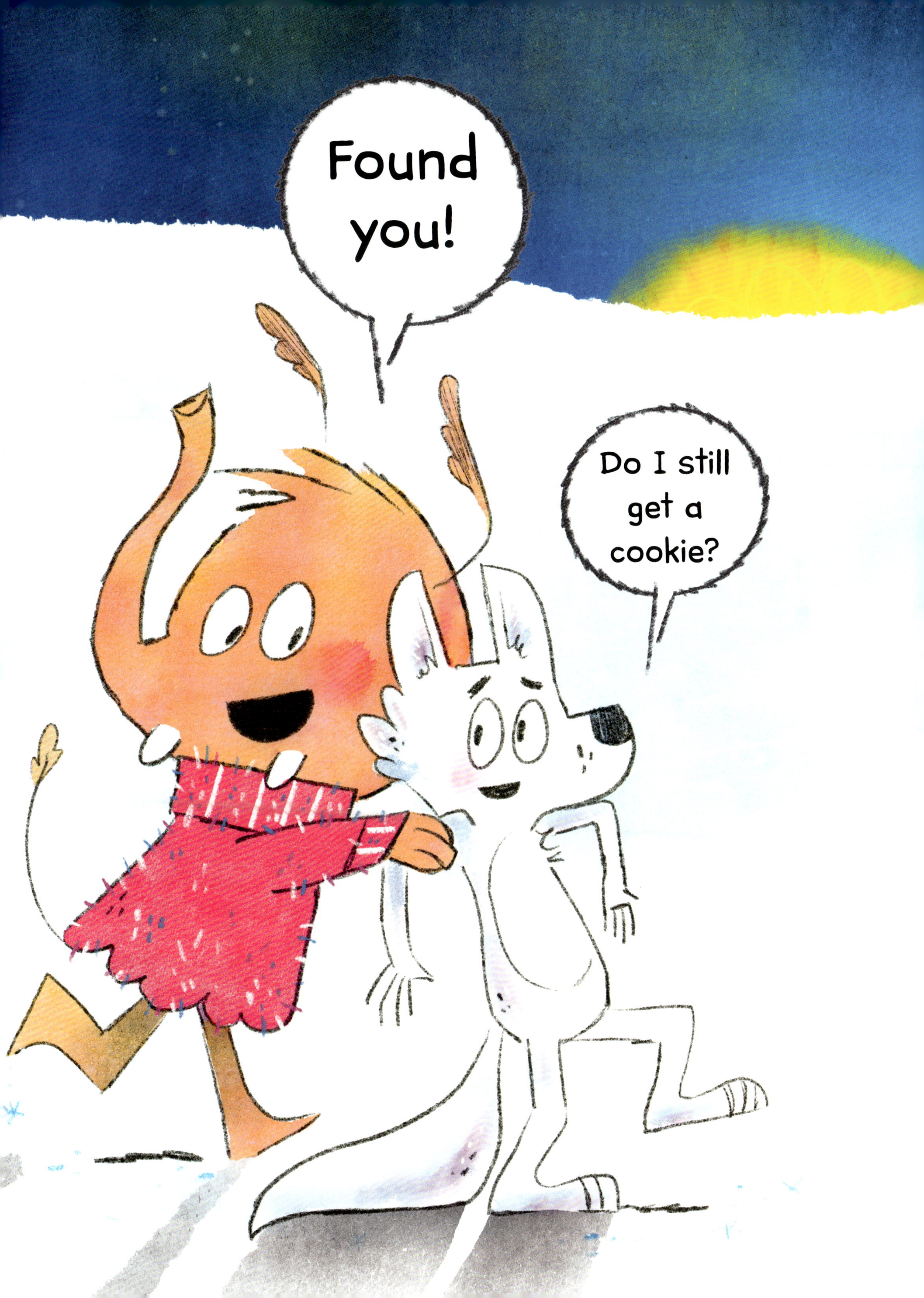
Found you!
Do I still get a cookie?

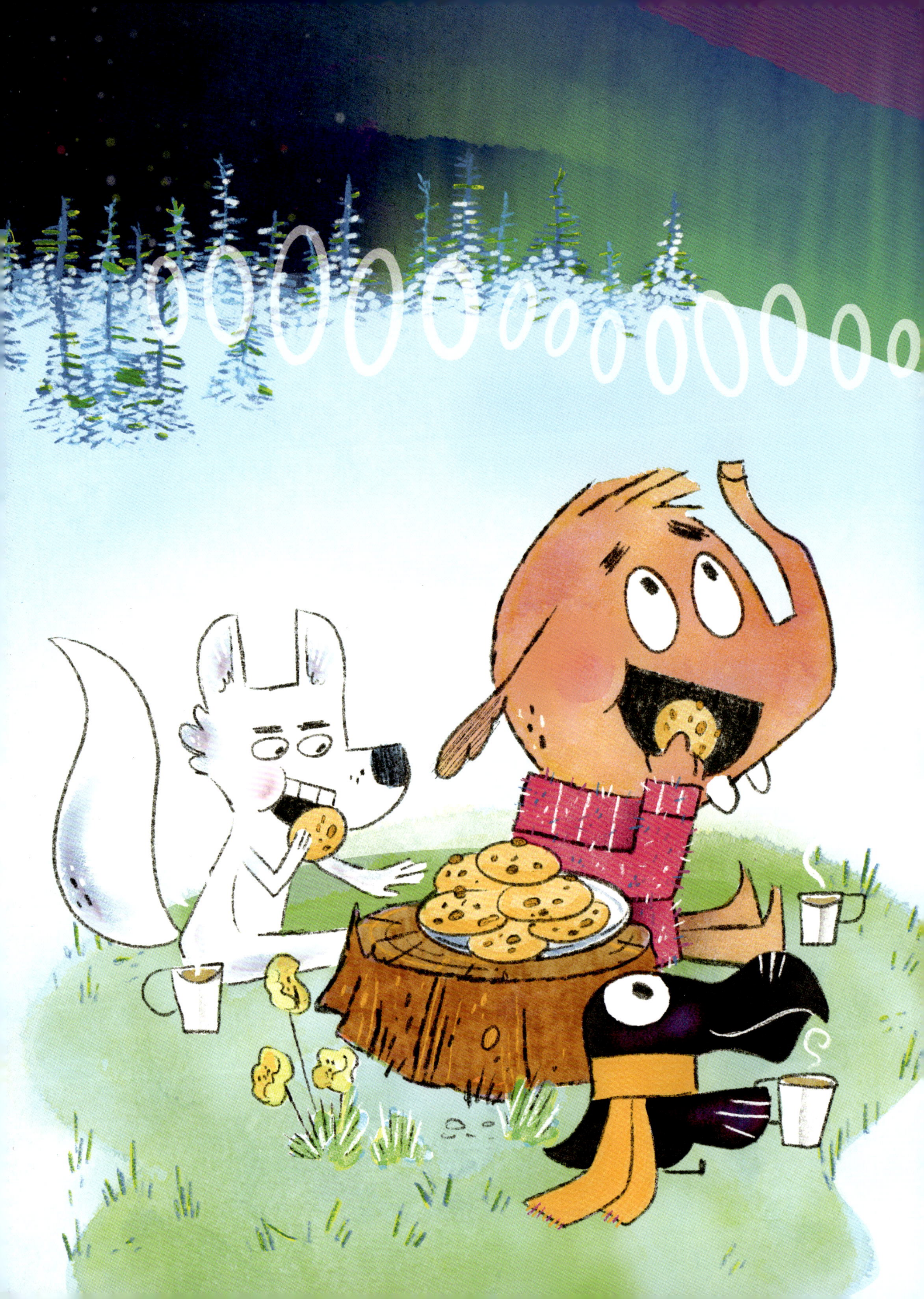

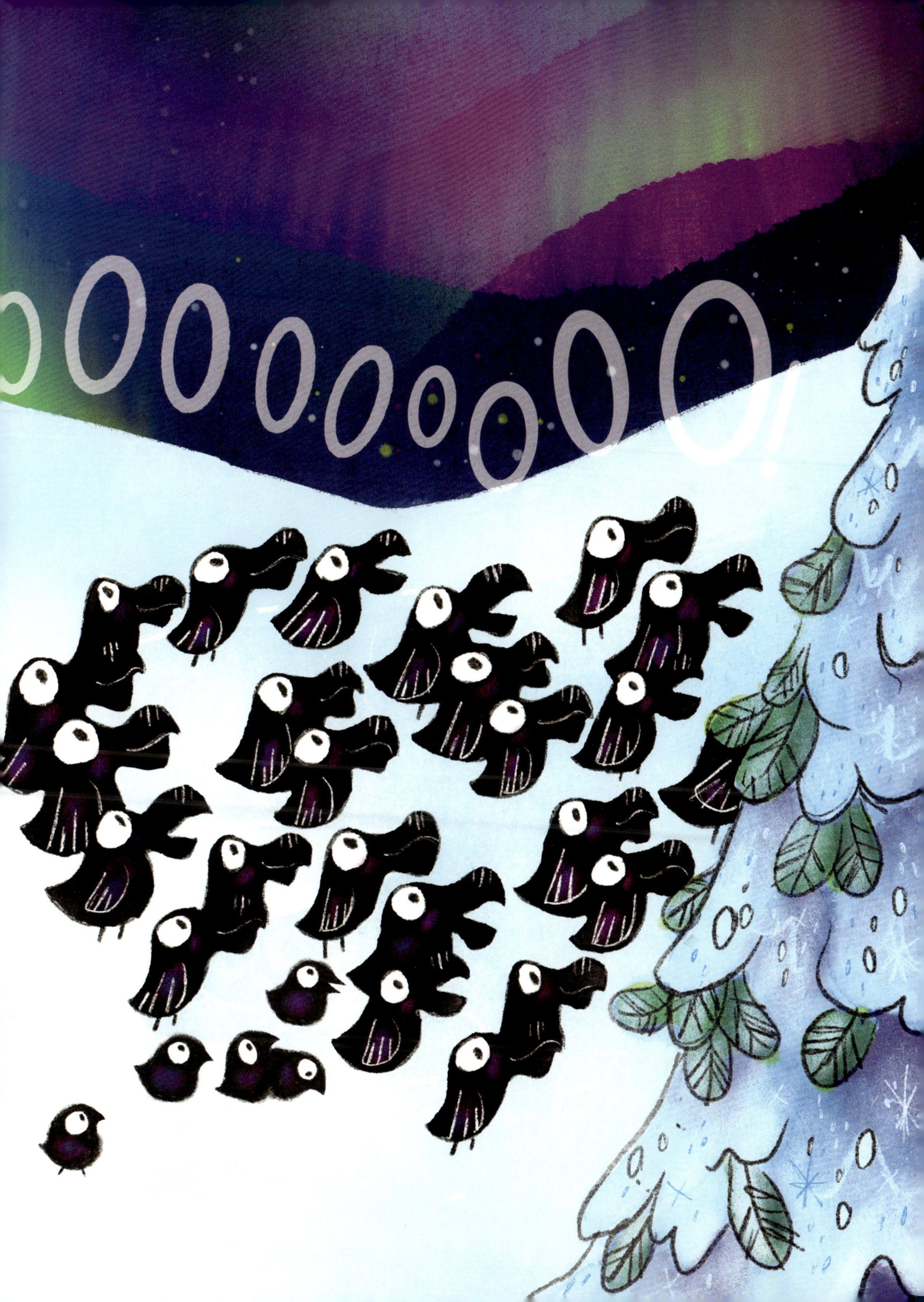
OOOOOOOOO!

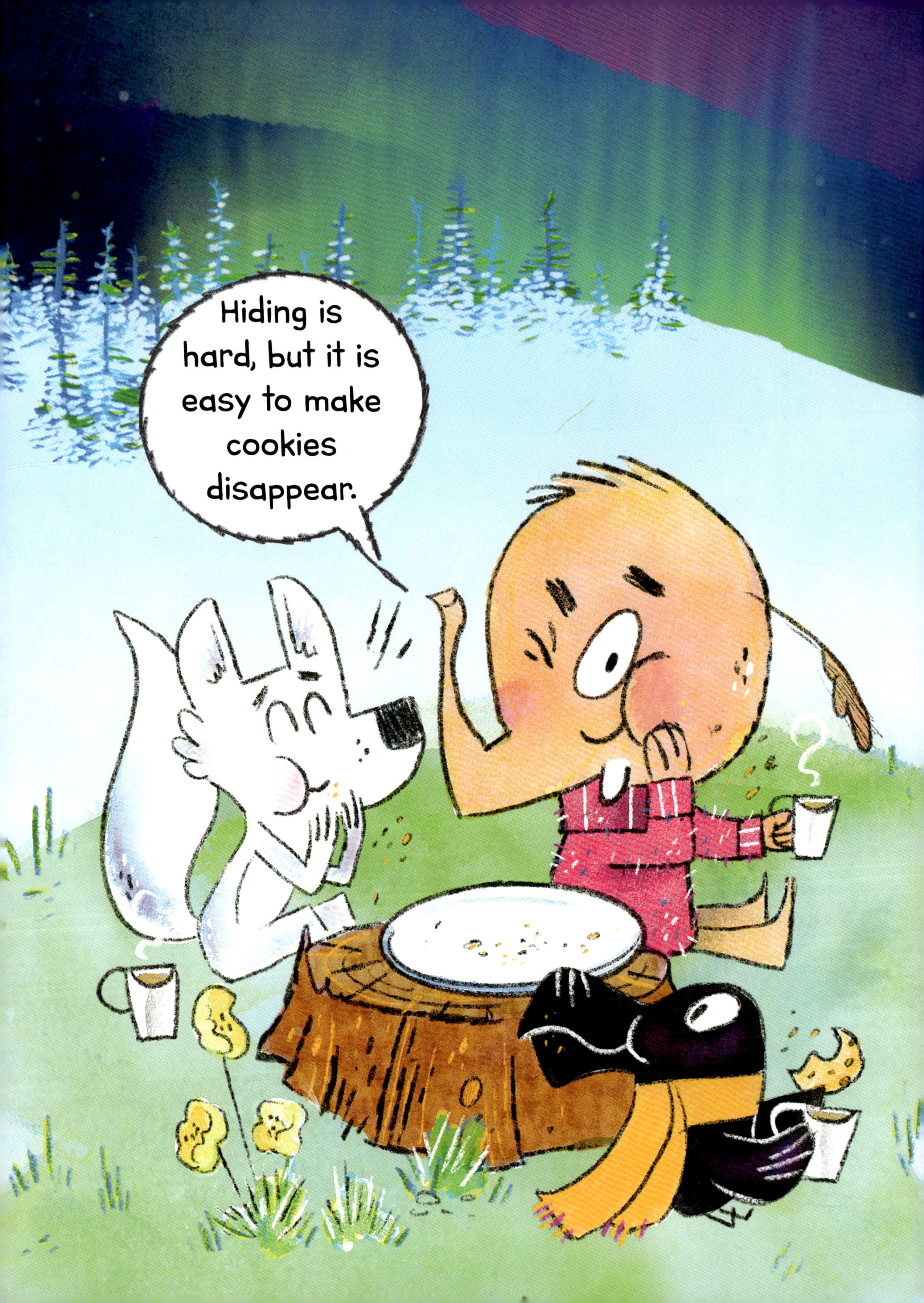
Hiding is hard, but it is easy to make cookies disappear.